Also by Diana Wynne Jones

Archer's Goon
Black Maria
Castle in the Air
Dogsbody
Fire and Hemlock
Hidden Turnings
The Homeward Bounders
Howl's Moving Castle
The Lives of Christopher Chant
The Magicians of Caprona
A Tale of Time City
Who Got Rid of Angus Flint?
Wild Robert
Witch Week

Eight Days of Luke

Diana Wynne Jones

MAMMOTH

First published in Great Britain 1975
by Macmillan London Ltd
Published 1992 by Mammoth
an imprint of Mandarin Paperbacks
Michelin House, 81 Fulham Road, London SW3 6RB

Mandarin is an imprint of the Octopus Publishing Group,
a division of Reed International Books Ltd

ISBN 0 7497 1225 2

A CIP catalogue record for this title
is available from the British Library

Printed in Great Britain
by Cox & Wyman Ltd, Reading, Berkshire

J116,937   £2.99

CONTENTS

For Colin

I THE FIRST TROUBLE

Unlike most boys, David dreaded the holidays. His parents were dead and he lived with his Great-Aunt Dot, Great-Uncle Bernard, their son Cousin Ronald and Cousin Ronald's wife Astrid; and all these four people insisted that he should be grateful for the way they looked after him.

David tried to be grateful. They sent him to a boarding-school which, as schools go, was not bad. Most holidays they arranged for him to go on an Educational Tour or to a Holiday Camp, and these were usually interesting enough to make up for David's not knowing any of the other boys who went on them. He did feel grateful when Cousin Ronald pointed out that he had opportunities which few other boys were given. But when he was at home in Ashbury and not on a Tour or Camp, he found it much harder to be grateful. And the older he grew, the harder he found it.

This particular summer no Tour or Camp seemed to have been arranged. Aunt Dot usually sent David a post-card before the end of term to tell him what Tour he was going on, and this time no postcard had come. David's heart sank a little on the way home, when he thought about it; but he was in a very cheerful mood and did not think about it much. He had taken five wickets for four runs in the match against Radley House, and had capped this by bowling his own games master middle stump, first ball, in the Staff match. It was enough to make anyone cheerful. Cousin Ronald was interested in cricket. He could tell Cousin Ronald all about it.

The railway work-to-rule meant that David had to wait two hours for a train in Birmingham, but he was so happy thinking just how he would tell Cousin Ronald about those wickets that he did not mind at all. He merely bought some bubble-gum and sat cheerfully chewing as he thought.

When his train drew in among the red houses of Ashbury, however, his heart sank another notch or so, and by the time he had changed from the Wednesday Hill bus to the Lockend bus, he was feeling definitely depressed. But as he stood up to get off the bus, he remembered that the Clarksons lived at the corner of the road, and cheered up a little. The Clarksons were the only children near and they were both younger than David, but they liked cricket and they were not bad fun, considering. The only trouble was that Aunt Dot said they were vulgar. David could never see why. He thought, as he climbed off the bus, that it was a habit of Aunt Dot's to call things vulgar—like Kent at school calling everything spastic—and it didn't mean a thing.

As he turned the corner, David took a look over the Clarksons' front gate. There was none of the usual clutter of bicycles lying about, and someone had weeded the front drive and planted a lot of useless flowers. That was ominous. David's heart went down another notch. He walked on up the road and opened the gate to Uncle Bernard's big red house, where there were never any weeds, or bicycles, and lines of geraniums were drawn up like guards on either side of the drive. David went up the steps and opened the front door and the smell of the house hit him. David had lately developed a theory that the sense of smell was much more important to the human race than anyone believed. The house smelt thick and dampish, of polish and old cabbage, the most dismal smell David knew. Like a proof of his theory, his heart went down about seven notches with a rush.

The hall was empty. This meant that, because of the railway work-to-rule, his trunk had not arrived yet. That was a nuisance. David's cricket-bat and the only pair of trousers that still fitted him had been in that trunk. It meant borrowing a bat and being stuck with short, tight school trousers until it arrived. He was rather sadly looking at the empty space in the hall where his trunk usually stood, when the door of the study opened. Cousin Ronald, balder and stouter and busier-looking than ever, came hurrying out, and with him came a gush of cricket-commentary from the radio in the study.

David remembered his six triumphant wickets. "Oh, Cousin Ronald, do you know what!" he said happily.

Cousin Ronald seemed dumbfounded. He stopped in his tracks and stared at David. "What are *you* doing here?" he said.

"It's holidays. We broke up yesterday," David said. "But do you know what—?"

"Oh, this is too bad!" Cousin Ronald interrupted peevishly. "And I suppose they've sent you home early because of some blasted epidemic and we'll all catch it now."

"No. Honestly," protested David. "It's just the end of term." He was beginning to lose all his joy in telling Cousin Ronald about those wickets; but it was too fine not to tell, so he tried again. "And do you know—?"

"It *can't* be the end of term!" said Cousin Ronald. "Not already, boy."

"Well, it is," said David.

"What a confounded nuisance!" Cousin Ronald exclaimed, and plunged back into the study again and shut himself and the cricket-commentary away inside it.

More than a little dashed, David went slowly away upstairs, trying not to feel miserable, trying to think about the cricket books in his bedroom. He came across Uncle Bernard on the first landing. Uncle Bernard did not seem to see David. He just tottered away to the bathroom looking frail and vague. David was heartily relieved. When Uncle Bernard noticed him, he always noticed the colour of David's fingernails, the length of his hair and the fact that his tie was comfortably in his pocket. It was much better not to be noticed by Uncle Bernard. David turned thankfully to go up the second flight of stairs and found Aunt Dot's tall figure coming down them.

"David!" exclaimed Aunt Dot. "Whatever are you doing *here*?"

"It's the holidays," David explained once more. "We broke up yesterday."

"Broke up *yesterday*!" said Aunt Dot. "I thought there was another week to go. It was extremely thoughtless of you not to let me know." Since David knew that the school always sent Aunt Dot a list of terms and holidays, he said nothing. "What a nuisance!" said Aunt Dot. "Well, since you're here, David, go and wash and I'll see Mrs Thirsk. Supper's in half an hour." She came on downstairs. David, knowing what a point Aunt Dot made of politeness, stood aside to let her pass. But Aunt Dot stopped again. "Good gracious, David!" she said. "Whose clothes are you wearing?"

"No one's," said David. "Mine, I mean."

"They've shrunk abominably," said Aunt Dot. "I shall write to the school and complain."

"Oh, please don't," said David. "It's not the clothes—really. I think I grew very fast or something."

"Nobody grows that fast," Aunt Dot decreed. "Those clothes were a good fit at Easter. You must go straight upstairs and see if you have anything else to wear. You

4

can't come to supper looking like that." And she sailed away downstairs.

David went on up to his bare, tidy bedroom. While he searched for clothes, he could not help forlornly wondering whether any of his school friends were having such a cheerless homecoming as he was. He rather thought that most of them had parents and brothers and things who were actually glad to see them. Some of the lucky so-and-sos even had dogs. David would have liked a dog above all things. But the thought of Uncle Bernard being asked to countenance a dog was almost frightening.

The only clothes he could find were smaller than the ones he had on. When Mrs Thirsk rang the gong, David was forced to go down to supper as he was. He met Mrs Thirsk in the passage and she looked him over with utter contempt.

"You do look a proper scarecrow," she said. "Your Uncle's going to have something to say about that hair of yours, if I know anything about anything."

"Yes, but you don't," said David.

"Don't what?" said Mrs Thirsk.

"Know anything about anything," said David, and he escaped into the dining-room, feeling a little better for having annoyed Mrs Thirsk. He had been at war with Mrs Thirsk from the moment he came to live in Uncle Bernard's house. Mrs Thirsk hated boys. David loathed every inch of Mrs Thirsk, from her blank square face to her blunt square feet. So he smiled a little as he slipped into the dining-room.

The smile vanished when he found Astrid there. Astrid was sitting beside the french window with her feet up, because, as everyone knew only too well, her health was bad. Astrid was quite pretty. She had fairish hair and big blue eyes, but her face was always pale and peevish, or it would have looked prettier. She dressed very smartly and told everyone she was twenty-five – she had been telling everyone this, to David's certain knowledge, for six years now.

At the sight of David, she gave a cry of dismay. "Never tell me you're back already! Oh, this is *too* bad! Ronald, you might have warned me!" she said, as Cousin Ronald came in.

Cousin Ronald was carrying a sheet of paper which David recognised as the list of holiday dates that the school had sent last autumn. "It came as a shock to me too," he said. "But they do seem to give the twentieth here."

"But you told me the twenty-eighth!" Astrid said indignantly.

Aunt Dot came in at this moment, with her diary open in front of her nose. David drifted away to the other end of the room. "Ronald," said Aunt Dot, "I have the end of term down here clearly as the twenty-eighth. Why was I misinformed?"

"Trust Ronald to get it wrong!" said Astrid. "If we have to miss going to Scarborough because of this, I don't know what I shall do. One of my heads is coming on already."

David, having no wish to hear any more about Astrid's head, reached out and gently twiddled the knobs of the radio on the sideboard. He was in luck. An announcer said: "Now, cricket. England in the Third Test are—"

"David!" said Aunt Dot. "People are talking. Turn that off at once."

Sighing, David turned the knob and silenced the announcer. But, at the same moment, Cousin Ronald hurried across the room, saying irritably: "I tell you I've no idea how it happened!" and snapped the radio on again.

"Five wickets for fourteen runs," said the radio.

"Quiet," Cousin Ronald said severely. "I have to know how England are doing against the Australians."

To David's secret indignation, no one made the slightest objection. Everyone stopped talking while the radio told them that England were 112 for eight when rain stopped play. By this time Uncle Bernard had tottered in, still frail from finding David had come home, and Mrs Thirsk was bringing in a tray of thick brown soup. Everyone sat down and began to eat. The thick brown soup tasted thick and brown.

David was very quiet and very careful of his manners. He did not want Aunt Dot to notice he was still in the same clothes, and he did not want Uncle Bernard to notice him at all. For a while he was lucky. Uncle Bernard and Astrid were busy with their usual contest to see who could be illest. Uncle Bernard began it by asking Astrid in a gentle, failing voice how she was.

"Oh, not too bad, Dad-in-law," she answered bravely. "It's only one of my heads this evening. How are you?"

"I never complain," said Uncle Bernard untruthfully, "but I am forced to admit that my lumbago is very troublesome tonight – though it's these fluttering pains in my chest which are the greatest nuisance."

"I get those too," said Astrid. "Dr Ryder gave me some tablets for them, but they've made no difference. I've been fluttering away all afternoon. Do they make you breathless? I can hardly breathe with them."

"I gasp for air all the time," retorted Uncle Bernard, gently and sadly. "My lungs have been in a bad way for years."

"Oh, so have mine!" cried Astrid, not to be outdone.

At this stage in the contest, David had awarded Astrid four points, and Uncle Bernard three, with a bonus-point to Uncle Bernard for never complaining. He rather hoped Astrid would win for once.

"I don't know how I shall get through the summer," Astrid said. David gave her another half-mark for that. "These shooting-pains in my shoulders just get worse too." That was another full point, making Astrid 5½. "Particularly," she said peevishly, "as it looks as if we aren't going to Scarborough after all."

She looked at David then, and David, terrified that Uncle Bernard was now going to notice him, finished his soup as quietly as he could and wished he had not given Astrid that extra half-mark. But Uncle Bernard was moving in to score heavily and had no attention to spare for David just then.

"My dear," he said, "I was always against your going to Scarborough. You'd never stand the journey." That made another bonus-point. "And for myself," said Uncle Bernard, "you could take me to Scarborough any number of times and it would do me no good. It would do me no good even if I lived there permanently. No – I prefer to live out my few remaining days quietly here in Ashbury."

That made a good eight points. Uncle Bernard had flattened Astrid and sat back to enjoy his victory. Astrid had not a word to say, but Aunt Dot, who was never ill and had no patience with anyone who was, snapped crossly: "I must say, Bernard, I wish you'd told me before that you didn't want to go to Scarborough."

"My dear, how could I, when I knew a holiday would give you such pleasure?" said Uncle Bernard, scoring a further bonus-point for martyrdom and self-sacrifice – though David rather thought that the contest was now over and it was against the rules to go on scoring. But then, he remembered, Uncle Bernard never did play fair.

Meanwhile, Mrs Thirsk took away the soup-bowls and handed out plates of thick brown meat covered with thick brown gravy. David, nibbling it, wondered why people ever complained of the meals at school. School food never tasted this bad, and there was always plenty of it. Mrs Thirsk had never been known to provide enough for a second helping. David thought that perhaps she knew one helping was all anyone could take. Here he looked up and saw Uncle Bernard staring at him. Having polished off Astrid, Uncle Bernard was about to begin on David.

David tried to prevent him, by saying brightly to Aunt Dot: "Aunt Dot, may I go round and see the Clarksons after supper?"

"No, David," Aunt Dot said, with satisfaction. "I'm glad to say those dreadful Clarksons have moved at last. They tell me the new people are a very much better class of person."

"Oh," said David. He felt as if his last hope of enjoying this holiday had now gone. But hope dies hard. "Have the new people any children?" he asked despairingly.

"Good heavens no!" said Aunt Dot. "The Frys are an elderly couple Mr Fry retired some years ago." David said nothing. The last hope was truly gone. There was nothing to do but sit and wait for the various miseries in store for him. And they were not long coming. "David," said Aunt Dot, "I thought I told you to change your clothes."

David tried to explain that he had now no clothes that fitted him any better. Aunt Dot swept his explanation aside and scolded him soundly, both for growing so inconsiderately fast and for arriving in advance of his trunk. It did no good for David to point out that people of his age did grow, nor to suggest that it was the railway's fault about the trunk. "When I want your opinion," said Aunt Dot, "I shall ask for it. This is most vexing. And tomorrow is Sunday, so that it will be Monday before Astrid can take you into town for new clothes."

This brought Astrid and Cousin Ronald out against David too. "No one," said Cousin Ronald, "no one objects less than me to spending money when it's necessary, but this is sheer waste, David."

Since David was now goaded to the point where he wanted to say that Cousin Ronald always, invariably, objected to people spending money, it was perhaps fortunate that Astrid got in first.

"Town always brings on my head!" she complained. "And shops make me feel faint. You might say you're grateful, at least, David."

"I am. Truly," David protested. "But I can't help growing."

All this while, Uncle Bernard had been hovering on the edge of the action, waiting for an opening. Now, just as Mrs Thirsk came to bring pudding, he pounced. "Growing," he said. "And I suppose you can't help your hair growing either? You must have it cut at once, boy." The odd thing about Uncle Bernard was that when he attacked David he never seemed in the least frail or ill. "Hanging round your ears in that unmanly way!" he said vigorously. "I'm surprised they haven't made you have it cut at school."

Mrs Thirsk shot David a malicious, meaning look, and David was naturally forced to defend himself. "The other boys all have hair much longer than this," he said. "No one minds these days, Uncle Bernard."

"Well I do mind," said Uncle Bernard. "I'm ashamed to look at you. You'll have it all off on Monday."

"No," said David. "I—"

"*What*?" said Uncle Bernard. "Do you have the face to contradict me? Boys do not decide the length of their hair, let me tell you. Their guardians do. And boys do not contradict their guardians, David."

"I'm not really contradicting," David said earnestly. Because Mrs Thirsk was there, he was desperately set on winning, but he knew that he dared not seem rude or ungrateful. "It's just that I want to grow my hair, Uncle Bernard. And it'll cost less money if I don't have it cut, won't it?"

"Money," said Uncle Bernard unfairly, "is no object with me when it's a question of right and wrong. And it is *wrong* for you to be seen with hair that length."

"Not these days," David explained politely. "It's the fashion you see, and it really isn't wrong. I expect you're a bit out of date, Uncle Bernard." He smiled kindly and, he hoped, firmly at Uncle Bernard, and was a little put out to hear Astrid snorting with laughter across the table.

"I never heard such a thing!" said Uncle Bernard. Then he went frail and added pathetically: "And I hope I shall never hear such a thing again."

David, to his amazement, saw that he was winning. He had Uncle Bernard on the run. It was so unheard of that, for a moment, David could not think of anything to say that would clinch his victory. And while he wondered, Mrs Thirsk turned his success into total failure.

"Yes," she said, "and did you ever *see* such a thing as this, either?" Triumphantly, she placed a small mat with crochet edging in front of Uncle Bernard. In the middle of the mat, very thoroughly stuck to it, was a wad of something pink and rather shiny, with teeth-marks in it.

Uncle Bernard peered at it. "What is this?" he said.

"David can tell you," said Mrs Thirsk, throwing David another malicious look.

Uncle Bernard, frail and puzzled, looked up at David.

"It's chewing-gum," David confessed wretchedly. How it had got stuck to the mat on his dressing-table, he could not imagine. He supposed he must have put it down there while he was hunting for clothes. But he knew it was all up for him now.

"Chewing-gum? In *my* house!" said Uncle Bernard.

"How simply filthy!" said Aunt Dot.

Astrid and Cousin Ronald closed in again then too, while Mrs Thirsk, looking like the Triumph of Righteousness, briskly planked a plate of stiff, cold chocolate pudding in front of David. Such of it as David managed to eat tasted as thick and brown as the rest of supper. As the row went on, as all four of his relations continued to clamour how disgusting he was and Mrs Thirsk to shoot smug looks at him, David resolved bitterly, vengefully, that if it was the last thing he did, he would tell Mrs Thirsk how rotten her food was.

It ended with David being sent up to bed. By that time he was quite glad to go.

II THE SECOND TROUBLE

The next day was hot and sunny. David got out of bed deciding that he would walk the three miles to the recreation ground after breakfast. There were almost certain to be boys playing cricket there, and a little artful hanging around fielding stray balls should earn him a game quite easily. He was half dressed when Mrs Thirsk came in. She was carrying an armful of clothes.

"Your Aunt Dot had me look these out for you," she said. "Your Cousin Ronald is too well-built for them these days. The trousers won't fit too bad if you turn them up round the waist. You can hold them up with a belt, can't you?"

David eyed the armful with horror as Mrs Thirsk dumped it on the bed. "I suppose so," he said, and decided he would rather die than wear Cousin Ronald's cast-offs.

"And don't say you will and then not wear them," said Mrs Thirsk. "I know you. You'll do what your Aunt wants for once, you will."

"All right," said David.

"It had better *be* all right, or I'll tell your Uncle," said Mrs Thirsk turning to go.

By that, David knew he was condemned to wear the things and misery made him angry. "Your food isn't," he said to Mrs Thirsk's back.

"Isn't what?" demanded Mrs Thirsk, turning round quickly.

"Isn't all right. It's horrible. I never tasted such horrible stuff," said David.

Mrs Thirsk's blunt face went purple. She said not a word, but she slammed the door as she went out. David laughed.

He stopped laughing when he saw himself in Cousin Ronald's clothes – though he was afraid that most other people would laugh their heads off. The trousers were far too loose, belt them as he would, and the large fawn sweater flared out over them like a ballet-skirt. Cousin Ronald had been what Mrs Thirsk called well-built most of his life. David blushed when he looked in the mirror. The only comfort was that the wide trousers were not at all too long – it was pleasant to think that he was suddenly the same height as Cousin Ronald and going to end up taller – but the rest of him was so grotesque that he knew he would have to give up going to the recreation ground. He dared not show himself to anyone looking like this.

He was so ashamed of his appearance that he dashed down to the dining-room before anyone else was up and – in a great hurry to get away before Astrid or someone came in and started to laugh at him – shook all the toast out of the toast-rack on to the tablecloth. He put butter on all of it and marmalade on half, and quantities went on the cloth because he was in such a hurry. He arranged it in a stack that he could carry, seized the radio from the sideboard to provide entertainment, and made off with the lot through the french window to the end of the garden where he could keep out of sight. There was a tall hedge there. Behind the hedge was a steamy compost heap with baby marrows growing on it and a spade stuck in the compost, and a strip of gravelly ground where Cousin Ronald always meant to have a carpentry shed. Beyond that was the high brick wall that ended the garden.

There David sat, with his back against the compost heap and the radio among the marrow-plants, and spent the kind of morning most people would rather not spend. It got very hot in the sun, and David was able to take off the fawn ballet-skirt sweater for an hour or so; but the gravelly space was quite without interest. David saw forty-two birds and listened to the morning service, a review of records, a concert and to someone promising to tell him about sport in the afternoon. Then the dinner-gong went, and he had to hurry to put the radio back so that Cousin Ronald could hear the news during lunch.

Lunch produced a scene far worse than the night before. It started with Aunt Dot coming in, followed by Mrs Thirsk, followed by Astrid.

Mrs Thirsk was saying: "And you may ask him why there was no toast, but what I want to know is why was there marmalade all over my clean tablecloth."

"Yes indeed," said Aunt Dot, and she turned ominously to David. "David," she said, and then – though this was clearly not what she had been going to say – "Good gracious! Whose clothes are you wearing?"

"Cousin Ronald's," said David, very much ashamed, but also rather glad of the diversion.

"Good gracious!" said Aunt Dot again.

Before she could begin on the tablecloth, Astrid sniffed piercingly and asked in her most complaining way: "Whatever is this dreadful smell?"

This made Aunt Dot pause and sniff too. "You're right," she said. "There *is* a most peculiar smell." To David's secret pleasure, both she and Astrid looked accusingly at Mrs Thirsk. David felt it confirmed his theory about the human sense of smell.

Mrs Thirsk backed to the door. "I'll go and fetch lunch, Mrs Price," she said primly, and made off.

"David—" began Aunt Dot, but this time it was Uncle

Bernard who interrupted by tottering in and saying, in his most failing voice:

"What is producing this vile smell, my dear?"

"We don't know," said Astrid.

"David—" Aunt Dot began for the third time.

But Cousin Ronald bustled in with a sheaf of papers in his hand and hurried over to the radio. "Quiet, please. I must hear the news." He reached out to switch on the radio, gave a throttled sort of shout, and dropped his papers. "What's this? Where has this radio *been*? Look! *Look* at it!" He picked it up in both trembling hands. A cloud of green and blue flies rose with it, flatly buzzing. Then, to David's acute dismay, a wad of brown smelly stuff gently detached itself from the base of the radio and sank on to the sideboard. It was followed by another. The flies sank after both wads, as if they were relieved to see them.

There was a nasty silence. Then all four of David's relations turned to look at him. "David!" they said, with one voice. After that, they said a great deal more. Lunch was held up while they said it, and then held up further while David took the radio and the wads of compost outside and some of the flies went with him. But most of the flies were of the opinion that the compost was still on the sideboard somewhere, and they stayed to look for it, maddening everyone, throughout lunch.

By the time David returned to the dining-room, Mrs Thirsk, as if she were trying to prove David's point, had served up thin grey meat in thin grey gravy and everyone else had started to eat it. David started to eat it too, wishing it could be magically transformed into fish and chips, and discovered that the rest of them were discussing the important question of how they were to spend next week in Scarborough now that David had come home earlier than they expected.

"What are we to do?" wailed Astrid. "I did so need this break."

"I detest cancelling bookings," agreed Aunt Dot.

"Oh, there's no real problem," said Cousin Ronald. David agreed with him. To his mind, there was no problem at all, and his heart warmed to Cousin Ronald. He thought he must certainly get Cousin Ronald to himself after lunch and tell him about those wickets at last. Cousin Ronald had the right ideas. "Look at some of these," said Cousin Ronald, passing his papers round. "It's not easy to find something at such short notice that doesn't involve considerable outlay, but I think it can be done. The one you've got, for instance, Mother."

"*T. W. Scrum M.A.*" read Aunt Dot off her paper. "*Holiday Tutorials in Elementary Mathematics*. Starting next Tuesday, I see. Quite reasonably priced, but it says board and lodging extra, dear."

"And no doubt a terrible bill for books," quavered Uncle Bernard, frail at the mere thought, scanning the paper he held. "This Cruise doesn't start till next month."

"Here's a Camp that might do," said Astrid. "Oh, no. It says for under tens. David's older than that, isn't he?"

"Of course I am," said David. No one seemed to hear.

"I think Scrum's our best bet," Cousin Ronald said jovially, and Aunt Dot agreed with him.

In growing outrage and dismay, David listened to them planning – just as if he were not in the room – to get rid of him by sending him to do Maths with Mr Scrum until the end of August. Cousin Ronald had gone into it very thoroughly. He assured them that Mr Scrum was the best and cheapest way of disposing of David. David revised his opinion of Cousin Ronald. As for the others, he had no opinion of them to revise. He bore it until he heard Uncle Bernard say: "Yes, I think so too. David's Mathematics are very weak."

"They are not!" David said indignantly. Then, realising that it would not do to annoy anyone any further, he said as politely as he could: "I'm quite good at Maths, Uncle Bernard. I came third in my form this term."

"Ah, but why didn't you come *first*?" said Cousin Ronald. "We'll settle for Scrum, then, shall we?"

"Let it be Scrum," said Aunt Dot decidedly.

David saw his fate being sealed and became frantic. "No, you needn't," he said loudly. Everyone turned angrily towards him. David made an effort to sound polite and reasonable, but he had to try so hard that his voice came as loud and careful as a radio announcer's. "It's quite simple really," he said. "Why don't you all go to Scarborough and just leave me here?"

"Oh indeed?" said Uncle Bernard. "And what do you propose doing in our absence?"

"Fill the house with compost and marmalade, I expect," said Astrid.

"No," said David. "That was a mistake. I'd be very careful, and I'd be out all day playing cricket." An idea came to him as he spoke. It struck him as a brilliant one. "I tell you what – you could buy me a bicycle."

"You'll be asking for your own car next," said Astrid. "Will you want a Rolls, or could you make do with a Mini?"

"Out of the question," pronounced Aunt Dot.

"No, it isn't," David said eagerly. "A bicycle would cost much less than going to Mr Scrum. I thought you'd leap at the idea, really. It's three miles to the recreation ground, you see."

"Get this clear, David," said Cousin Ronald. "You are going to Mr Scrum for your own good, and not to any recreation ground on any kind of conveyance."

"I don't want to go to Mr Scrum!" David said desperately.

"Why not?" Astrid said, laughing. "He may be very nice."

"How do *you* know?" said David. "How would *you* like to go to Mr Scrum?" Astrid's mouth came open. Before she or anyone else could speak, David plunged on, again trying so hard to be polite that his voice came out like an announcer's. "It's like this, you see. I hate being with you and you don't want me, so the best thing is just to leave me here. You don't have to spend lots of money on Mr Scrum to get rid of me. I'll be quite all right here."

There was a long and terrible silence. One of the shiny green flies buzzed maddeningly three times up and down the table before anyone so much as moved. At last, Cousin Ronald, red right up to the bald part of his head, pushed back his chair with a scrape that made David jump, and stood up.

"Get out," he said, with fearful calmness. "Leave this room, you ungrateful brat, leave your lunch, and don't dare come back until you can speak more politely. Go on. Get out."

David stood up. He walked to the door, which had somehow moved several miles off since he last came through it, and when he finally reached it, he turned and looked at them all. Three of them were sitting like statues of themselves. Cousin Ronald was still standing up, glaring at him. David saw that he really was the same height as Cousin Ronald, and that made him feel much less frightened of him, but much more miserable.

"I took five wickets against Radley House last week," he said to Cousin Ronald. "You couldn't do that."

"Get out," said Cousin Ronald.

"And I bowled our games master. Middle stump," said David.

"*Get out*!" said Cousin Ronald.

"First ball," said David, and he went out and shut the

door very carefully and quietly behind him, much as he would have liked to slam it. Mrs Thirsk was coming up the passage from the kitchen, perhaps to bring the pudding, but more likely because she had heard something interesting going on. "Thin grey pudding!" David said loudly. But he could not meet Mrs Thirsk face to face because there were now tears in his eyes. He slipped out of the side-door instead and went running up the garden with great strides, until he reached the private space between the wall and the compost heap.

It was baking hot there. The air quivered off the compost. David stripped off the ballet-skirt sweater – which served to dry his face – and squatted down anyhow in the middle of the gravel. He could not remember having been so angry or so miserable before. For a while, he was too angry and miserable even to think.

His first real thought was to wonder why he had not seen before that all his relations wanted was to get rid of him whenever they could. He supposed that was why they made such a point of his being grateful – because they looked after him when they did not want him in the least. And he wondered why he had not realised before.

His second thought was to wish he could go away and live on a desert island. Knowing that was impossible made him so miserable that he had to walk about and scrub his eyes with the back of his hand. Then he thought he would like to have the law on his relations. But they had not done anything he could have the law on them *for*. The judge would say they had treated him well and he ought to be grateful.

"Oh, I *hate* being grateful!" David said. And he wished his relations were wicked, instead of just ordinary people, so that he could do something awful to them.

Then he thought of the way they were sending him to Mr Scrum, and he wanted to do something awful to them anyway. Something to make sure that they were miserable for every moment they spent in Scarborough. Suppose he put a curse on them? Yes, that was it. He had read a rather pointless book last term, in which the boy put a curse on someone and it had worked. He would do the same to Uncle Bernard, Aunt Dot, Cousin Ronald – specially Cousin Ronald – and Astrid.

David roved up and down the hot space thinking what to put. And he had another idea. He would not curse them in English, because that was too ordinary, so ordinary that it might not even work. But he had read somewhere else that if you gave a set of monkeys a typewriter each and let them type away for twenty years or so – wouldn't they get tired of it in five minutes? David broke off to wonder – anyway, they typed away and ended up accidentally typing the complete works of Shakespeare. In the same way, surely, if you just said any sounds that came into your head, wouldn't you, mightn't you, end up by reciting a real rattling good curse that would make it snow in Scarborough all next week and perhaps bring Cousin Ronald out in green spots into the bargain? And if it did, it would have the advantage of being an accident, and not truly David's fault at all.

It seemed worth trying. For the next twenty minutes or so, David walked up and down the hot gravel, from compost to wall and back, muttering words and mouthing what he hoped were strange oaths. When he found a combination that sounded good, he stood still and recited it aloud. Each time he felt secretly a little foolish, because he knew perfectly well it had made no difference to his relations at all. But it was very satisfying all the same, and he went on.

At last he found the best combination of all. He could really almost believe it was words, fierce, terrible words. They asked to be said. And they asked to be said, too, in an important, impressive way, loudly, from somewhere high up. David climbed to the top of the compost heap, crushing baby marrows underfoot, and, leaning on the handle of the spade, he stretched the other hand skywards and recited his words. Afterwards, he never remembered what they were. He knew they were magnificent, but he forgot them as soon as he said them. And when he had spoken them, for good measure, he picked up a handful of compost and bowled it at the wall.

As soon as he did that, the wall started to fall down.

III LUKE

It was like an earthquake. It is a horrible feeling to have caused an earthquake. The wavering and heaving were to some extent under David's feet, and the compost shifted and quivered like quicksand. That would have been enough to send David leaping down from it. But he could see that the wavering and heaving was stronger near the wall. He knew the wall was going to come down and that it was his fault. He tried to run towards it.

"No, no!" he said. "Stop it! I didn't mean it!"

The solid ground came up in ripples under his feet and made him stumble. In front of him, the wall rippled too. He could hear the bricks grinding as they swayed up and down. The top of the wall made a crazy outline against the hot blue sky, wagging up and down, with bricks coming loose and lifting, then banging back into place again, and mortar spurting from between them. After that, there was so much dust and mortar that he could hardly see the wall, and he had to hold his arm over his head against the rubble raining down on him. The heaving underfoot went fiercely on. The wall could take no more and fell, backwards from David, in three slow, sulky bangs, into the garden behind Uncle Bernard's, and set loose even more dust as it went.

The next second, the gravel was covered with angry orange flames, pale and vicious-looking in the sun and dust. David backed out from them desperately, until his shoulders hit the hedge and held him up. But the flames had gone by then. They just flared through the dust as if someone had dropped a match in a pool of petrol, and then went out. David was sure his curse had punctured a gas-main. He looked the heaving ground over hurriedly, to try and locate the leak before going to confess and get help. He saw a round thing, something like a pipe and at least as thick as his arm, writhing among the rubble, and he thought it was a gas-pipe. It was covered with an ugly mosaic pattern which glittered in the sun. There were others, too, further off, and if David had not known they were gas-pipes, he would have sworn they were snakes – snakes somehow swimming in the rippling ground, as if it were water.

Then the thing nearest David surfaced, shaking clattering small stones off its blunt head, and saw David. It reared up as tall as he was, hissing furiously. David found himself face to face with a very large snake indeed, with a head as flat as Mrs Thirsk's feet, a forked flicking tongue, and yellow eyes which seemed to be made of skin. He could see its fangs, and the poison sacs at the top of them, and he was sure there was poison dripping from those fangs.

David lost his head. He made a frantic sideways dash along the hedge and seized the spade from the compost. The snake struck after him and missed. It was still half under the gravel, which hampered its movements, fortunately for David, and the ground was not heaving so much now. David turned round with the spade in both hands, and hit the snake a hearty smack with it. He did not kill it, but he made it recoil. So he hit it again. Meanwhile, at least two other snakes were moving towards him, slowly and with difficulty, as if the ground were getting harder every second. David hit the first snake again, and then aimed a swipe at the next two, to discourage them. But the first snake reared up again as he did so, and he had to concentrate on that.

He would never have managed alone. But, while David beat away at the first snake, he heard somebody else busily battering at a snake in the distance. There was so much dust and confusion still, that he never saw the person clearly while the battle lasted. He assumed it was Cousin Ronald at first. Then he caught glimpses of a shape much taller and thinner than Cousin Ronald's and he thought it must be Aunt Dot. But he had little time to think. The ground was hardening all the time and he simply hammered the snakes back into it. If he hit them often enough, he discovered, they went back under the gravel and stayed there. The real trouble was to do it before the next snake could reach him, and that was where the other person helped. It was not until David had smacked the last length of the last snake well and truly into the earth that he realised this person was a complete stranger.

They stood looking at one another in the settling dust, David leaning on the spade and the stranger propped on the hoe he must have fetched from the shed beyond the hedge. David was shaking all over. The stranger was panting rather, but not in the least upset. He looked jaunty. He even laughed a little, as if snakes were a bit of a joke. He was not as tall as David had thought—only about David's height—and he seemed a year or so older than David.

"Thanks," David said to him gratefully.

"Thank *you*," replied the stranger, jauntily smiling. "I'm Luke. Who are you?"

"David Allard," said David. "I live in that house there. Do you—?" He meant to ask if Luke lived in the house beyond the broken wall, but he turned to point as he said it and after that he could think of nothing but what a hideous mess it was. The wall was in three long heaps— an utter ruin, lying on the neatly mown grass of the neat

25

and respectable orchard belonging to the neat and respectable house David could just see down among the trees. David thought it was a miracle that nobody had come out of that house – or Uncle Bernard's – with loud shouts of fury. Or not yet. "Oh dear," David said miserably.

"A bit of a ruin, isn't it?" Luke agreed.

"Yes, and I did it," David said. "I shall get into trouble." Which was putting it mildly, he thought.

Luke laughed, and jumped on to the nearest heap of wall to look at it more closely. "Did you really do this?" he said. "How?"

David followed Luke over to the wall, thinking that Luke must be a trespasser and nothing to do with the neat and respectable house after all. He was wearing cast-off looking clothes, much like David's, and he was covered with brick dust, cement dust and what seemed to be soot. And it was plain he did not care two hoots about the broken wall. He sat himself down on a convenient heap of bricks and patted another to show David where to sit too.

"Explain," he said, and folded his arms, ready to listen, with a very engaging look of interest. Luke had a sharp and freckly face, under the dirt, and a burn or something on one cheek, probably from those sudden flames. His hair seemed to be red. At any rate, he had those kind of red-brown eyes that only go with red hair. David rather took to him.

"I did it trying to curse," David confessed, and sat down too, though he could not help taking a nervous look at the respectable house first.

"Don't worry. They're out, or they'd have been up here raving half an hour ago," Luke said, which proved to David that he was certainly only a trespasser. "Now, explain. Whom were you cursing?"

"All my horrible relations," David said. It was a relief

to talk about it. He told Luke how his relations did not want him, how they were planning to send him to Mr Scrum so that they could go to Scarborough, about Mrs Thirsk, the food and the chewing gum, and about the row at lunch. Luke listened sympathetically, but it was when David came to the cursing part that he grew really interested.

"What did you say?" he asked. "Can you remember?"

David thought, and was forced to shake his head. "No. It's gone. But I suppose it was some kind of curse if it knocked the wall down."

Luke smiled. "No. It wasn't a curse."

"How do you know? It brought out a load of snakes too, didn't it?"

"But it wasn't a curse, all the same," said Luke.

David was a little annoyed. For one thing, Luke could not possibly know, and, for another, although it would have been a relief not to have uttered a curse after all, it was plain to David that his words had had a powerful effect of some kind. "What was it then?" he said challengingly.

"Unlocking words. The opposite of a curse, if you like," Luke said, as if he really knew. David said nothing. He thought Luke was trying to make him feel less guilty about the ruin they were sitting on. Luke smiled. "You don't believe me, do you?" David shook his head. "Oh well," said Luke. "But they were, and I'm truly grateful to you. You let me out of a really horrible prison." He smiled happily and pointed with one slightly blistered finger to the ground under the wall.

This was too much for David, who, after all, had been there to see that nothing but flames and snakes had come from the ground. "Pull the other leg," he said.

Luke looked at him with one eyebrow up and a mischievous, calculating look on his filthy face. He seemed to be deciding just how much nonsense David could be brought to swallow. Then he laughed. "Have it your own way," he said. "But I am grateful, and I'll do anything I can in return."

"Thanks," David said disbelievingly. "Then I suppose you can help me stand this wall up again."

Luke looked at David in that shrewd and mischievous way again. "I might," he said. "Shall we see what we can do?"

"Oh do let's," David said sarcastically.

Luke jumped up briskly. "Come on, then. You take the other end of this and help me lift it." He stooped and put his hands to a section of brickwork, where the wall had come down still cemented together. "Come on," he said. "Don't look so glum about it."

So David, feeling hopeless about it, got up slowly and wandered to the other end of the joined piece of wall. He put his hands to it and found the bricks coming loose as he touched them.

"Heave!" Luke said cheerfully.

David heaved, not very hard. But he must have heaved harder than he thought, because he managed to raise the whole section. Luke lifted his end, and together they carried a whole chunk of wall, grinding and bending, and laid it down in one piece by the compost heap.

"There, you see?" said Luke, and went jumping gaily back across the bricks. "Now this bit."

In a remarkably short time, they had all the complete sections of wall laid out in order on the gravel. When these were moved, they found there had been a tree growing up against the back of the wall – part of the neat orchard – and the wall had crushed it as it went over. They looked at it, Luke laughing and David glum. Luke shook his head.

"It's dead," said David.

"Yes, but we can fake it a bit," Luke said. "You pull that branch straight."

They spread the tree out until it looked the right shape for a tree again. Then Luke lifted it in his arms and thumped the broken trunk into the soft ground until it stood upright. Its leaves were withering and wilting still, but it looked as if it were growing.

"Can't bring the dead to life, I'm afraid," said Luke, "but they might think it died from natural causes, with luck."

Then they rebuilt the wall. David had never imagined it could be so easy. True, they worked hard and sweat trickled through the dirt on their faces, but they laughed and whistled as well, and the wall grew in leaps and bounds. As they worked, David came to like Luke more and more. He was fun. He made jokes all the time, and no difficulty seemed to dismay him. Some of his jokes were complete nonsense, mostly because he chose to keep up the pretence that David had let him out of prison. "My chains," he said, as they staggered under the largest section of wall, "were a good hundred times heavier than this." Then again, when they got to the most difficult part, which was slotting the newly rebuilt wall into the jagged ends of the walls at the sides of the garden, Luke said something odd. David was doing the slotting, while Luke held the wall tilted for him. He could see Luke's muscles standing out in knots.

"Are you sure you can hold it?" David asked.

"Nothing like so heavy as a bowl of venom," Luke panted cheerfully. David laughed.

Once the wall was slotted in, they were finished. It was not perfect. The upper courses of bricks wandered up and down a little, and because they had used no cement, there were places where you could look through to the orchard. But it stood solidly. David and Luke were very proud of it.

"Not bad, considering neither of us ever built a wall before," Luke said. "What shall we do now?"

David looked at his watch and found it was nearly supper time. "I shall have to go in," he said mournfully. "They get furious if I'm late." He was very dejected. He remembered he was in disgrace and about to be sent to Mr Scrum on Tuesday. It was too bad, now that he had met Luke. "Can you come out after supper?" he asked, thinking he must see as much of Luke as he could while he had the chance.

"Of course," said Luke. "Whenever you want. Just kindle a flame and I'll be with you."

"Meet you here then," said David.

"As you like," said Luke. David turned to go and Luke, laughing, but trying to look solemn, raised one hand like a Redskin salute. "Farewell, oh my benefactor," said he.

"Oh do shut up about that!" David said, and ran down the garden laughing.

IV THE THIRD TROUBLE

David was filthy. He had to wash and climb into more of Cousin Ronald's wide cast-offs before he dared to go down to supper. The odd thing about washing in a hurry is that soap and water only loosen the dirt. Most of it comes off on the towel afterwards. David looked rather nervously at the reddish-black smears on Mrs Thirsk's bright white towel, but he was in too much of a hurry to do anything about it. The gong had gone before he started to wash.

He hurried downstairs, thinking about Luke and Luke's odd jokes. If Luke had not come along, there was no doubt David would at this moment be crawling downstairs in the most hideous state of guilt, wondering how he was going to confess to having cursed a wall down. As it was, he felt much better. Rebuilding the wall had wiped away his misery and also the horror of the way the curse had worked. He thought of the flames and the snakes, but all they did was to remind him of Luke's joke about kindling a flame. David grinned as he came to the bottom of the stairs, because someone – Astrid probably – had left a box of matches on the stand beside the gong. David slipped them into his pocket as he passed. If Luke wanted him to strike a match as a signal, then he would. But it was no good asking for matches. That would only remind his relations to forbid him to have them.

He went into the dining-room. Astrid was saying: "And my leg never left me in peace, the whole afternoon."

"*Both* my legs," said Uncle Bernard. Then he saw David in the doorway and abandoned the contest. David walked to his place and sat down in a silence heavier and nastier than any he had known. It was clear the row was still going on. Unless, David thought rather nervously as he picked up his soup spoon, they had found out about the wall and were angry about that now. The soup was burnt. David could see black bits floating in it. It tasted burnt.

Cousin Ronald broke the silence at last by saying reproachfully: "We are waiting to hear you say sorry, David."

"Sorry," David said, wondering why they could not have told him that straight away.

There was another heavy silence.

"We want to hear you apologise," said Aunt Dot.

"I apologise then," said David.

"I don't call that an apology," said Uncle Bernard.

"Well, I said sorry and I said I apologise," David pointed out. "What else do you want me to say?"

"You might take back your words," suggested Astrid.

"All right. I take them back," David said, hoping this would now mean peace. But he thought as he said it that it was just like Astrid to say the silliest thing of the lot. "How can you take back words anyway? I mean, once you've said them they've gone, haven't they, and—?"

"That will do," said Cousin Ronald. There was more silence, broken by the reluctant clinking of spoons, during which David began to wish that his curse had really been a curse and working at this moment. Then Cousin Ronald cleared his throat and said: "David, there is something we have to tell you. We have decided, solely on your account, not to go to Scarborough after all. We shall stay here, and you shall stay with us."

David could hardly believe his ears. "You mean not go to Mr Scrum?"

"I mean not go to Mr Scrum," said Cousin Ronald.

"Oh, *brilliant*!" said David. His relief and delight and gratitude were so enormous that he could almost have hugged Cousin Ronald. "Thanks!" What a good thing it had not been a curse! Now he was free to do what he liked and see as much of Luke as he could. "That's marvellous!" David beamed round the table at his relations. They looked solemnly and reproachfully back.

"David," Cousin Ronald said reproachfully, "I hope you realise that we are all making a considerable sacrifice for your benefit. Scarborough meant a lot to us. We will say no more about your rudeness at lunch, but what we would like to hear from you in return is a proper expression of thanks to us for all we have done for you."

Under such a speech as this, most people's gratitude would wither rather. David's did. "I *said* Thanks," he protested. "But I'll say it again if you like."

"What you say is beside the point, child," Aunt Dot told him austerely. "All we want is that you should feel in your heart, honestly and sincerely, what it means to be grateful for once."

"Then what do you want me to do?" David asked rather desperately.

"I sometimes think," said Uncle Bernard vigorously, "that you were born without a scrap of gratitude or common good feeling, boy."

"But I *do* feel grateful," said David. "I'm ever so grateful for not going to Mr Scrum, really!"

"Grateful for not going to Mr Scrum!" said Astrid. "Listen to him! Does it matter to him that we're deprived of our holiday? Not a bit. David wouldn't turn a hair if I were to drop dead at his feet."

"Yes I would. Anyone would," said David. He thought

about what he would feel if Astrid did actually chance to drop dead at his feet. "I'd be very surprised, and I'd think you were pretending at first. But when I began to believe it I'd get a doctor to make sure you really were dead."

"Aren't we chivalrous!" Astrid said crossly.

"No, I'm not," David said, as Mrs Thirsk came in with the next course. "But you're not a damsel in distress."

Astrid went very red and glared at David all the time Mrs Thirsk was handing out plates with dark meat on them covered with dark gravy. The meat was dark because it was burnt. It tasted terrible, so terrible that even Uncle Bernard noticed.

"This meat is burnt," he said fretfully. "I don't think it's eatable."

Everyone except David thankfully laid down their knives and forks. David was so hungry after rebuilding the wall that he had practically eaten all his anyway, and it seemed a shame to leave the rest.

"That boy has no discrimination," said Uncle Bernard, as Mrs Thirsk came back to see what was the matter.

"Mrs Thirsk—" began Aunt Dot.

"I can't *think* how it happened!" said Mrs Thirsk. "It was beautiful five minutes ago. And when I came back after taking the soup, there it was, black! And it was on the table. No heat near it."

"It has been near a very great heat for a considerable time, I should say," Uncle Bernard said, prodding it. "I can't find your explanation adequate, Mrs Thirsk."

"Adequate or not, it's the plain truth!" said Mrs Thirsk. She gave David a malignant look as she said it, as if she would have liked to put the blame on him if she could.

"The soup was burnt too," said Astrid.

"That was right as rain when it left my kitchen," claimed Mrs Thirsk. "You may say what you like, but I can't understand it." And for five more minutes, at the top of her voice, Mrs Thirsk went on not being able to understand it, either the soup or the meat.

"Let's have the pudding anyway," said Cousin Ronald hungrily, and Mrs Thirsk went angrily away to get it.

The pudding was burnt too, and Mrs Thirsk could not understand that either. "It was right as rain," she said. "Good as gold it was. Now look at it!"

"Oh let's not have all that again," said Cousin Ronald. "Bring us some bread and cheese, and do try not to burn that if you can."

Luckily, it was beyond Mrs Thirsk's skill to burn bread and cheese, so everyone began hungrily to eat that. David was pleased. It looked as if he might, for once, get enough to eat in this house. The bread was a little stale, but wonderfully filling, and the cheese was the strong orange kind which David particularly liked.

"You know," Cousin Ronald said, taking nearly half the strong orange cheese, "Mrs Thirsk is a rotten cook, Mother. Couldn't we get someone else?"

That was a lovely idea. David's heart once again warmed towards Cousin Ronald, even though he had taken so much cheese.

"I invite you to try to get someone else, Ronald," said Aunt Dot, finishing that idea for good and all. "David, please stop that unmannerly stuffing. Even if you can't find it in your heart to be grateful, you need not pretend that we starve you."

This was the signal for all four of them to turn on David again. The truth was that David's announcement over lunch had made them all feel very much ashamed, and they could not forgive him for it. So they told him all over again how ungrateful he was, until David could bear it no longer.

"I don't know why you think I'm not grateful," he

said. "I *was* grateful, until you all started going on at me. But I'm not any longer. Nobody could be."

"Well!" said Aunt Dot.

"Let's go to Scarborough after all," said Astrid.

Cousin Ronald pushed his chair back and stalked to the french window. "That settles it," he said. "I'm going into the garden." And he went.

The other three stayed where they were. David was wishing heartily that it was actually possible to take back one's words, when Mrs Thirsk came in, ready to put herself in the right again at David's expense, bearing like a flag a white towel with red and black grime all over it.

"Look at this—" she began.

She got no further, because Cousin Ronald shot back into the room, groaning with rage, carrying something like a green sausage someone had stamped on. "My marrows!" he said. "Just look what this brat has done to my marrows!"

David was sent up to bed again. The one bright spot he could see, as he climbed the stairs and slammed the door of his room, was that Cousin Ronald had not noticed anything wrong with the wall. Otherwise, everything was horrible. It was just not fair. He was quite ready to be grateful, if only they left him alone – but that was the last thing they would do.

David sat on his bed and looked longingly at the window. Luke was probably waiting for him at the end of the garden by now. It was a hot, golden evening. Midges circled just outside, and swallows swooped in the distance. David thought of all the things he and Luke might be doing and was miserable. And because he had nothing else to do, he took out the box of matches and fiercely struck one. Serve them right if he burnt the house down!

Almost at once, he heard a faint thumping and rustling from outside the window. David was at the window after

36

the first thump. Luke was climbing up the creepers like a monkey.

"Oh, brilliant!" David said, and all his misery vanished.

Luke looked up as David spoke, rather red in the face, and grinned. The movement shifted his weight. "Help!" Luke said. There was a sharp ripping noise, and the creepers began leaning away from the house, carrying Luke with them. David leant out as far as he dared and seized Luke's desperately waving arm. After a good deal of heaving, he managed to pull Luke in over the window-sill, both of them laughing rather hysterically – the way you do when you have had a fright. "Thanks," said Luke.

"Look at the creeper!" David said, and both of them went off into muffled giggles again. The creeper was hanging away from the house in a great bush, and its leaves were turning a scorched and withered brown. David was secretly appalled at the mess, but Luke was not in the least worried.

"More faking necessary," he said. "Hang on to me while I get hold of it." So David gripped Luke round the waist and Luke leant as far out of the window as he could. Somehow, he managed to grab the creeper and hook it back on the nails it had been tied to, where it hung, still limp and brown and withered, it is true, but nothing like so obviously broken.

Then they turned back into the room, and David, to his horror, found the match he had struck lying on the floor still burning. He rushed and stamped it out.

"You see," said Luke, "you only have to kindle a flame to fetch me. Now, what's the matter? In trouble again?"

"I'll say I am!" said David. He gave Luke the history of supper, and Luke laughed. He laughed about the marrows, the towel and the burnt food. He lay comfortably on David's bed, with his dirty shoes on Mrs Thirsk's white bedspread, and laughed even when David said passionately: "I'm sick of having to be grateful!"

"Quite right," he said, scratching at the burn on his face, which seemed to be healing nicely.

"It's all very well to laugh," said David. "You don't have to stand them all going on at you."

"Oh, I know what that feels like," Luke said. "My family was just the same. But there's no sense in being miserable about it. Did you enjoy supper, by the way?"

"The cheese was all right," said David. "What Cousin Ronald left of it."

Luke chuckled. "I thought of burning the bread too," he said, "but I didn't want you to go hungry."

"Tell me another," said David.

"Seriously," said Luke, although David could see from his face he was joking again. "Mrs Thirsk deserved it. What shall we do now?"

"I suppose we could play Ludo," David suggested, looking mournfully at the scanty shelf of amusements by his bed.

"I don't know how to play Ludo," said Luke, "and I can see from your face that I shouldn't like it if I learnt. I've a better idea. Would you like to see some of my doodles?"

"What are they?" David asked cautiously.

"What I used to amuse myself with in prison," said Luke. "Look at that corner, where it's darker, and if you don't like them you can always tell me to stop. I can go on for hours."

Dubiously, David looked at the corner of his room. A tiny bright thing appeared there, coasting gently along, like a spark off a bonfire. It was joined by another, and another, until there were twenty or thirty of them. They clustered gently together, moved softly apart, combined, climbed and spread, and were never still for a moment.

It was rather like watching the sparks at the back of a chimney, except that these made real, brief pictures, lacy patterns, letters, numbers and stars.

"Not boring you?" said Luke. David shook his head, almost too fascinated to wonder how Luke made the things. "Let's have a change of colour, though," Luke said quietly.

The bright things slowly turned green. The shapes they made now were stranger, spreading at the edges like ink on blotting-paper. Outside, it was getting dark. Luke's green doodles showed brighter and brighter. Then they went blue and clear, and made shapes like geometry, all angles.

David had no idea how long he watched. He stared until his eyes ached and he could see shapes even with his eyelids down. Every so often, Luke would make a quiet suggestion and the style of the doodles would change again. "Blood-drops," he would say. "Now some wild shapes." And the bright things in the corner altered. Luke had just made them purple when David fell asleep.

V THE FIRE

Luke must have climbed down the creeper while David was asleep. He was not there in the morning, anyway, and David felt very flat without him. The morning was made no livelier by Cousin Ronald's refusal to let David near a radio. David wanted to hear the Test Match as much as Cousin Ronald, but Cousin Ronald, saying that any radio David went near became covered with compost, took all three radios with him into the study and shut the door in David's face.

There was nothing for David to do but unpack his trunk, which arrived soon after breakfast. His cricket bat, when he came to it, did not seem as large as he remembered, and all the clothes were rather small.

"That means new everything," Astrid said, sighing. "We'll be all afternoon. My head will be splitting in this heat, but I know you won't care *how* I feel."

"Yes I will," David said truthfully. When Astrid had a headache, she was always more than usually spiteful, so it was natural to hope that her head would not split.

"Thanks for nothing," Astrid retorted and climbed into her Mini, jangling bracelets and flouncing her handbag. "Don't rush to get in, will you?"

"You have to unlock the door first," David said patiently, wondering how he was to get through this shopping expedition without being rude to Astrid.

It was very difficult. Astrid could find nowhere to park her Mini. She drove from place to place, grumbling, while the inside of the car became hotter and hotter. Astrid announced that she felt faint and said she would drive home again. She did not do this, however, because she was almost as much afraid of Aunt Dot as David was. Instead, she drove to a very distant car-park, and they set out to walk back to the shops. Astrid's feet hurt her.

"There are shooting-pains in my insteps," she said. "Do you think I've dislocated my toe?"

"No. It's because you wear such silly shoes," David explained.

"I've had about enough of your cheek!" Astrid said, and marched on very fast and upright to prove David wrong.

David trotted after her, sweating in the heat and dodging among the crowds on the pavement. He longed to be elsewhere – preferably by the compost heap, meeting Luke. Then he began to wonder if it was really true that he only had to strike a match to bring Luke. He knew it was only Luke's nonsense really. He could prove it, if he wanted, by striking a match here, in the middle of Ashbury, where Luke could not possibly turn up. David did not want to. He wanted to pretend that Luke was the one extraordinary thing that had happened in this exceptionally miserable holiday. But, by the time Astrid had told him twice not to dawdle and three times more about her feet, David had reached the stage where he wanted to prove that everything was flat and ordinary and horrible, just because everything so obviously was.

While they were waiting to cross a street, David turned aside, fetched out the box, struck a match, and then had to throw it flaring in the gutter, because Astrid told him sharply not to dawdle and he had to walk on across the street.

"Hallo," said Luke, strolling across beside him with his hands in his pockets. "Why are you looking so hot and bothered?"

David beamed at him. Life was suddenly quite different. "I just hate shopping," he said. "And she keeps on telling me to walk quicker."

"Which cat's mother's she?" said Luke.

"Astrid," David said, giggling.

Astrid turned round when she heard her name. "What are you at *now*?"

"I've met a friend," David said gaily. "Can Luke come with us, Astrid?"

"Well, really!" said Astrid, and she looked Luke over in a most unfriendly way. This, David thought, was unfair, because Luke looked remarkably clean and spruce today. His red hair was tidy, his freckled face was clean, and the burn on his cheek hardly showed at all.

Luke, however, held out his hand to Astrid, smiling most politely. "How do you do, Astrid?" he said, and contrived to sound well-brought-up and dependable saying it.

"Mrs Price to you," Astrid said haughtily. But she shook hands with Luke and did not look as haughty as she sounded. "Well, come along if you're coming," she said.

When they reached the first shop, Luke stood, looking rather wondering, among the lines of coats and stacks of shirts, while David tried things on. David and Astrid disagreed, as David had known they would, about what to buy. David's idea of good clothes was loose comfortable things that looked best grubby. He cast longing looks at a rack of jeans, and at cotton sweaters in interesting colours. Astrid's idea was something Aunt Dot would not disapprove of. She made David try on a suit with tight prickly trousers and asked the assistant for distasteful white shirts, with buttons.

"I don't like this suit," David said sadly. "It pricks. And I don't like those shirts either."

Astrid took hold of his elbow fiercely and led him out of the assistant's hearing. "I warn you David," she told him in a passionate whisper, "I shall do something dreadful if nothing's going to satisfy Your Majesty except red robes and ermine!"

"I'd be satisfied with jeans," David said hopefully.

"You ungrateful little—!" Astrid began, but stopped when she realised that Luke was standing just beside David. "I give up!" she said to them both.

"Quite right," Luke agreed cheerfully. "I don't think much of that suit either."

"What's wrong with it?" Astrid asked angrily.

"He looks like a penguin," Luke said.

Astrid looked at David, ready to deny it. But, in fact, the tightness and prickliness of the suit did make David stand in an awkward, stiff way, with his arms slightly out, very much like a penguin. "*Doh!*" said Astrid, and marched back to the assistant. David heard her say that they would leave the suit and just take the shirts, and could hardly believe his luck. He looked at Luke, and Luke gave him a smile of pure mischief.

This episode did not improve Astrid's temper. After the assistant had packed up the disagreeable shirts and they were leaving the shop, she said: "Now we shall have to go all the way to Trubitt's and I want no more nonsense. I've got one of my heads coming on already."

As David and Luke followed her, Luke said, out of the corner of his mouth: "How many heads has she got?" David doubled up with laughter. He could not help it. He staggered sideways across the pavement, howling and coughing, with packets of shirt sliding out of his arms in all directions.

Astrid, naturally, turned back, demanding to know what had got into him this time.

"I don't know," Luke said artlessly. Then, very

artfully, he added: "You know, Mrs Price, you look to me as if you've got a headache."

"I do?" said Astrid, forgetting David. "Well, as a matter of fact I have, Luke. Right over my left eye."

"Terrible," Luke said sympathetically. "How would it be if we were to go somewhere where you could sit down and rest for a while?"

"Oh, I'd give anything if I could!" said Astrid. "But we haven't time. I promised David's Aunt I'd buy him some clothes and—"

"You'll do it all the quicker for having a rest," Luke told her, kindly and firmly. "There's plenty of time. You take my arm and tell me where you'd like to go."

"You are a nice, considerate boy!" Astrid exclaimed. "But I'm not sure we ought."

Luke, with a soothing smile, held out his arm to her and winked at David – one small flicker of a wink that Astrid did not see. Astrid hooked her arm through Luke's and set off for the nearest cafe so quickly and thankfully that David got left behind. When he caught up with them at the door of the cafe, Luke was saying: "I quite thought you were David's sister. You look so young."

Astrid beamed at him, and continued to smile while they found a table and sat down. David sat down with them, rather thoughtfully. He was not sure that Luke was behaving quite honestly. Luke knew perfectly well that Astrid was not David's sister, because David had told him all about her yesterday. He was simply buttering Astrid up. David would have been annoyed, if he had not been pretty certain that Luke was only doing it to give David a more pleasant afternoon than he would have had otherwise.

Whatever his motives, Luke thoroughly enjoyed himself in that cafe. So did David. And, David suspected, so did Astrid too. The odd thing about Astrid was that, when

Cousin Ronald was not there to stop her, she loved spending money. She spent lavishly in that cafe. Luke's appetite was even larger than David's. He had five milk-shakes to David's three, and four ice-creams to David's two. Astrid ate one out of a plate of cakes, and then Luke and David finished them. David felt pleasantly full for the first time that holiday. Luke must have been nearly bursting.

Astrid continued to smile. And, instead of telling Luke all about her aches and pains, which David very much feared she would, she joked about both their appetites. "Are you sure that number of ice-creams will keep you going?" she asked. "It says *Banquets Arranged* here. How about it? Ten courses is a bit mingy, though, isn't it? Luke would starve. Should I just go out and get an ice-cream factory?"

"Why not?" said Luke.

"Well, it's fitting it into the Mini," said Astrid, and David was amazed at the difference being in a good mood made to her. He only remembered Astrid being this jolly three or four times, some years ago, when he had first come to live with his relations, and that had only been on rare occasions. Yet here she was, her face all pink with laughter, opening her handbag to take out a cigarette and taking a mock-guilty look round the cafe, as if Uncle Bernard might be there disguised as a waitress. Uncle Bernard classed cigarettes below bubble-gum.

"Don't tell on me, David," she said. "Have you got a match?"

David felt in his pocket for his matchbox, and was about to say that Astrid must not tell on him either; but, before he could fetch the box out, Luke leant forward and snapped his fingers at the end of Astrid's cigarette. There was a flame like a match-flame for a split second, and then the cigarette was alight. Astrid's eyes were wide with amazement beyond it.

"How ever did you do that?" she said through a cloud of smoke.

"A trick I learnt ages ago," Luke said modestly.

"I've never seen it done before!" said Astrid. Then, not unnaturally, she became very interested in Luke and asked who were his parents and where he lived. But Luke – to David's disappointment, because he would have liked to know too – was not telling. "But where *do* you live?" Astrid said cajolingly.

Luke smiled. "At the very tip of South America."

"Oh, you!" said Astrid.

Before Astrid could ask more, Luke began cajoling in his turn. In two minutes flat, he had persuaded Astrid to buy David comfortable clothes – a thing David knew he could not have done himself if he had talked for a month. Astrid agreed that the neat and comfortable clothes Luke was wearing would be far better for David than Aunt Dot's kind. But she stuck on the thought of Aunt Dot.

"Dot'll kill us both if we come back with those," she said. She thought about it, while David and Luke exchanged a rather hopeless look. "I tell you what!" Astrid said suddenly. "David, can you keep a secret?"

"Yes," said David.

"Then I'll get you some jeans and things if you swear to change into the other clothes for meals," Astrid said daringly.

David swore to do it. It seemed a small price to pay. Since Trubitt's was just across the road from the cafe, only half an hour later David was provided with clothes to suit him and clothes to suit Aunt Dot also. He and Luke, almost identically dressed, came galloping happily down the stairs from Trubitt's top floor, carrying numerous parcels and laughing like conspirators. And Astrid, despite her broken toe, shooting pains and various heads, came galloping after them in high good humour, saying: "Oh, I do love secrets!"

But, alas, the second floor of Trubitt's had a doorway hung with roses and labelled *Miss Ashbury*. Astrid paused.

"I say, you two," she said, "do you mind being angels and waiting just five minutes?"

David could hardly refuse. Luke, of course, said courteously: "Not at all, Mrs Price."

They spent the next half hour staring out of one of the long windows at the cafe opposite, while Astrid hurried about with armfuls of dresses behind them, in and out of the changing rooms.

"You know," David said to Luke, "you got her into too much of a good mood."

"I did, didn't I?" Luke agreed, rather mournfully.

"She likes spending money," David explained, and added, to cheer Luke up: "But I'm awfully grateful."

"You've no need to be grateful," Luke said, quite seriously for him. "None at all. You set me free, and it's only right that I should do anything I can for you in return. Honestly."

"Come off it!" David said, but he said it very uncomfortably, because he was beginning to suspect that it might be true.

Half an hour later still, they had decided that more fat people went into the cafe than thin ones; they had each scored two orange Minis; they had counted the windows in the office-block above the cafe and made them thirty-four each time; and Astrid had still not decided whether to buy six dresses or four dresses and a coat.

"I'm sick of this," said David. "I wish something interesting would happen."

"Such as?" said Luke.

"A robbery or a fire or something," said David.

47

"Anything we could look at. All that happens is people and cars."

"I could manage a fire for you," said Luke. "Would you like it if that block with thirty-four windows were to catch fire?"

"That would be brilliant," David said, laughing. "I just wish you could manage it."

"All right," Luke said quietly.

David was still laughing, when it struck him that the air outside was oddly misty. The office-block was dim and he could hardly see the traffic. He looked up to see where the fog was coming from, but the sky was blue and clear. The fog was rising up against it, thin and black and hot-looking above the office-block.

"Hey!" he exclaimed. "I think that building really is on fire!"

"Yes," said Luke. "It caught nicely."

David looked at him unbelievingly. Luke was staring intently at the building, with a gentle, coaxing smile on his mouth. His red-brown eyes were smiling in a different, vivid way, and moving up, slowly, over the building. "Luke!" David said sharply. As he said it, Luke's mouth opened in a little sigh of satisfaction.

"Ah!" said Luke.

A big cloud of black smoke rolled from the open windows above the cafe and, whirling round, like part of the smoke, were fierce orange flames. A bell began to ring in the building, loudly and continuously, and it brought people hurrying out of the cafe and the shops on either side. They turned to look up at the building, pointed and exclaimed and jostled. Then more people came out of the glass doors that led to the offices. These came pouring out, far more frantic and many more of them, treading on one another, pushing, spilling out on to the road, shouting, waving their arms and getting in the way of cars. One man's coat was smouldering and two people were beating it out for him. A lady stumbled and sat down in the gutter. In a matter of minutes, the road was in chaos, with people running all over it, cars stopped in zig-zags, a crowd gathering, and a policeman and two traffic wardens trying to move everyone off and not succeeding.

David looked at Luke. He was smiling, smiling, watching the building as if he were entranced. "Luke," David said.

Luke did not answer. Long flames were beating out of all the open windows. Where the windows were shut, David could see fire behind the glass, orange and whirling, like a sunset reflected back to front.

"Luke," said David, "I didn't mean—"

"Beautiful, isn't it?" Luke said raptly.

With a merry double blaring, a fire-engine swept down the street and stopped outside the building. Then another came roaring and blaring from the opposite direction. While the firemen jumped down and unreeled hoses, police cars arrived, blaring too, with blue lights flashing on top.

By this time, everyone else in the shop had realised there was a fire. Assistants and ladies shopping came crowding round David and Luke in great excitement.

"Just look at those flames! The *size* of them!"

"There's another fire-engine on its way. Look."

"We were in that very building only half an hour ago!" Astrid told people inaccurately.

"Just think of the cost of all that damage!" someone said.

"Oh," said someone else. "This has made my day!"

It certainly was exciting. David admitted that. But he was struggling with that sick, uncertain, itchy feeling you have when you know you have done something wrong. Flames were lashing from all but the top windows now, and those were smoking. Three hoses were going, in solid arches of water, but they only made the windows steam and splutter and had no effect on the flames. Luke was laughing gently, living in those flames, basking in their heat, and, David was sure, somehow whipping them up to greater power in spite of all the firemen could do. David had no doubt at all that Luke was a very strange person indeed and that Luke had made the fire to please him. That was why he felt so itchy and guilty.

The trouble was that David, particularly in the holidays, was so used to feeling guilty that he had come to ignore it whenever he could. He found himself pretending that the fire was nothing to do with him; that it was probably nothing to do with Luke either; and that, anyway, he had no influence over Luke. He had almost stopped at least the sick part of the feeling, when he looked up, because flames burst out of one of the top windows and across the roof, and flared into the sky against rolls of thick smoke. And he saw two office girls on the roof, scrambling towards a chimney and looking quite terrified. He caught one in the act of throwing away her silly, Astrid-type shoes in order to climb better, and he knew he must do something.

"Luke," he said, "I think those girls are stuck."

"Stuck?" Luke said vaguely. "Yes, I expect so. The stairs and the lift have gone. The roof's going in a minute."

The women round David saw the girls too, and began asking one another why somebody didn't *do* something. David took hold of Luke's elbow and shook him.

"Luke, could you stop this fire if you wanted?"

"Of course," said Luke, but his eyes were fixed on the heart of the building and he was not really attending.

"Then could you stop it now?" David said. "Those girls are going to be burnt."

Luke smiled absent-mindedly. "Little twits," he said. "They went to comb their hair first, then they panicked."

No doubt he was right. David thought they looked just that kind of girl. But it made no difference to the fact that they were hanging on to a chimney in a desperately narrow space between the flames and yelling for help. The firemen had put a ladder up against the next building, but there was clearly no chance of them reaching the girls.

"Luke," David said. "You can't bring the dead to life. Remember?"

Somehow, that seemed to be the right thing to say. Luke sighed, and the entranced look on his face altered, so that David could see he was attending.

"Luke," he said, "I want the fire out now."

Luke seemed surprised and rather hurt. "Don't you like it?" he said.

"I love it. It's brilliant," David said. "It's just those silly girls that have messed it up. Do put it out now. Please."

Luke smiled at him – a real, friendly smile, and not that strange, entranced one. "All right," he said. "Have it your own way." Regretfully, he looked across at the building again.

The fire began to die down at once. The flames shrank away from the roof, leaving a wide black trail. At the upper windows they seemed to stoop and cower. Then they were gone, leaving blank black windows, though there were sparks still, round the frames. Then the same happened at the next row of windows. By this time, a fireman was climbing across the roof towards the girls, and the women round David and Luke, who had hardly believed it at first, began to clamour.

"There, what did I tell you? They've got it under control!"

"I *knew* those girls would be all right!"

But, as the fire died down stage by stage, Luke's face grew sadder. David took his arm again and gave it a squeeze.

"Cheer up. It was a brilliant fire."

"Yes, it was, wasn't it?" said Luke.

VI MR CHEW

That evening, for the first time since he came home, David was not sent to bed early. Astrid was still in a good humour, and so busy telling Aunt Dot about the fire that she let Uncle Bernard score twenty-two points in the illness-contest without scoring one herself. That put Uncle Bernard in a good mood too. And Aunt Dot was pleased because David had come into supper looking as Aunt Dot thought boys should look. David could not resist giving Astrid a tiny flicker of a wink, like Luke's.

The only discontented one was Cousin Ronald. He was cross because it looked as if England was going to lose to Australia, and because his new gardener had not turned up. "Rang up this afternoon, if you please, and said he'd got a better job at Thunderly Hill," Cousin Ronald told them. "Of course I got on to the other chap straight away, but he can't come till tomorrow. At this rate the garden will be a wilderness by Wednesday."

He told them this several times. Nobody took any notice. So Cousin Ronald, peevish at being ignored, tried to pick a quarrel with David by making the incredible statement that they could say what they liked, but he knew Gleeson had been throwing in the overs before tea.

The reason why David did not contradict him and end up by being sent to bed was that he was too busy thinking about Luke. He thought of Luke working his dishonest miracle on Astrid, and he thought about the fire, and he came to two conclusions. One was that Luke did not operate by the same rules as other people. The other was that, if so, Luke was something of a responsibility. He was great fun, but David was going to have to be careful what he said to him in future. As for Luke's story about prison and being grateful, David still thought that might be a joke. But he was not at all sure now.

Whatever the truth was, David and Luke spent a splendid evening together. David went into the front garden after supper. He struck a match. And Luke came cheerfully in through the front gate. After that, they rambled round the neighbourhood. Luke was one of those who could not pass a yard, an old gate, or an empty house without seeing if they could get in. They found a dozen splendid places like this and returned tired, grubby and happy at David's bed-time. David went in through the front door. Luke swung himself up the creepers to David's window. David fell asleep watching Luke's doodles go, in a procession of dragons, across his bedroom wall.

Luke had said he was going, but he was asleep on the end of David's bed when David woke up the next morning. He had wrapped himself in the carpet and looked very comfortable.

David sat up gently, not to disturb him, and spent some while looking at Luke's sleeping face, wondering who and what Luke really was. He was very freckly. The burn on his face had quite gone now, which David thought was odd. He had an idea that burns usually took longer to heal. Another odd thing was that, now Luke was asleep, it was quite impossible to tell how old or how young he was. He might have been older than Cousin Ronald or younger than David. David thought first one age, then another, as he looked, until he remembered that, if he was certain of anything, it was that the usual rules did not apply to Luke. He wished Luke would wake up.

But Luke slept peacefully on, while David got up and

put on his jeans. David had to leave him there when he went downstairs, because, in order not to have to put on smart, prickly clothes, he had to have breakfast before Aunt Dot came down. He listened for the moment when Mrs Thirsk went along to the dining-room with the toast and dashed downstairs then. He meant to take toast back to his room and share it with Luke. But luck was against him. Cousin Ronald was in the dining-room, waiting for his porridge.

"If this new man doesn't turn up this morning," he told David, for lack of anyone better to tell, "I shall write to the papers. Sit down, can't you, boy."

David had to sit down, and to eat six slices of toast, while Cousin Ronald told him about England's position in the Test and all about how hard it was to get gardeners. Then, just as David was hoping to be able to go at last, Cousin Ronald picked up the newspaper.

"*Typists trapped on roof*," he read. "Oh, here's your fire, David!" David felt his face go red. For it *was* his fire, exactly. "*Thirty thousand pounds of damage!*" Cousin Ronald read severely. David shifted on his chair. "*Cause of fire still a mystery*, I see," said Cousin Ronald.

At that moment, David heard Mrs Thirsk going heavily upstairs, and he knew she was on her way to tidy his room. He wriggled all over his chair. Surely Luke would have the sense to climb out of the window or hide in the bathroom? What Mrs Thirsk would say to Aunt Dot and Aunt Dot would say to David about boys whose friends slept on the ends of their bed wrapped in good carpets did not bear thinking of.

Luckily, Cousin Ronald happened to glance out of the window. He jumped up irritably. "There's that blessed man at work on the dahlias already!" he said. "Why couldn't he come to the door as instructed?"

"Excuse me," David said thankfully and bolted, out of the room and upstairs two at a time.

His worst fears were realised. He heard Mrs Thirsk's voice from his room, and then Luke's. David set his teeth ready to take trouble and pushed open the door. Both of them turned to him. Luke looked harassed, almost frightened, but Mrs Thirsk did not seem as angry as she ought to have been.

"David," she said, "here's your friend fell asleep waiting for you, you greedy boy. You ought to be ashamed. Now just you take poor Luke downstairs and give him a nice bowl of porridge and some toast."

"Yes," said David. "Yes, of course." He realised that Luke had worked another miracle, this time on Mrs Thirsk. She was eating out of his hand – or rather, Luke was eating out of hers. But he could see she had given Luke a scare or he would not be looking so upset. "Was she furious?" he asked anxiously, as he and Luke went downstairs.

"No, not really," said Luke. "It's – look, David, can you help me get out of the house? And if you want to summon me, can you do it well away from here until he's gone?"

"Yes," said David, mystified. "But what's happened?"

Luke took hold of his wrist and pulled him cautiously over to the landing window. He pointed, but, David saw, he kept well away to the side of the window himself. David looked out, expecting – well, he hardly knew what he expected, except that it was something alarming. All he saw was the broad back of Cousin Ronald's new gardener, who was slowly weeding a flowerbed.

"See him?"

"The gardener?" said David. He turned back to Luke, wondering what was so alarming about a fat old gardener, and meaning to make a joke about it. Luke's face was narrow and hunted-looking and his eyes had gone very wide and golden. David saw he really was frightened. "Who is he?" he asked.

"Chew," said Luke. "I can't think how – but I couldn't get out of the window with him there. I'll have to get out by the front door, if you could keep him talking while I do. He's very stupid. If you just chatter, he won't suspect a thing."

"All right," said David, though it seemed a mystery that Luke should be afraid of someone so fat and stupid.

They came downstairs and met Astrid in the hall.

"Hallo, Luke!" Astrid said. "Nice to see you again. That fire's in the paper this morning. Did you see?"

Luke turned to Astrid with his most charming smile, but he gave David a nudge as he turned, to tell him to get out and distract that gardener. David went through the dining room, towards the french window. Halfway to it, he stopped short and nearly went back again. He heard Aunt Dot say, in her haughtiest voice:

"Just who is this person, Astrid?"

"Er – this is Luke," Astrid said, sounding rather guilty about it.

David thought that if Luke could charm both Astrid and Mrs Thirsk, he could probably handle even Aunt Dot. He sped on towards the french window and collided with Cousin Ronald coming in.

"Look where you're going, boy!" snapped Cousin Ronald.

"Sorry," said David. "Cousin Ronald, what's the new gardener's name?"

"Mr Chew," said Cousin Ronald. "Must be Chinese or something. Don't you go interrupting him."

David ignored that instruction. He scudded in long strides up the lawn and came to a rather sudden halt beside Mr Chew's great right shoulder. Mr Chew was not fat. He was wide because he was built on the lines of a gorilla, and the width was pure muscle. David no longer wondered why Luke was frightened when he saw Mr Chew's massive right arm, swathed in muscles and spread with rough black hairs, moving out towards a weed. Mr Chew's big horny hand hovered and then made a vicious jabbing plunge. The weed came up between fingers that looked capable of tearing up a tree. Mr Chew – or did you spell it Chou? David wondered – grunted, tossed the weed on a heap of others, and moved on to another.

"Good morning, Mr Chew," David said nervously. Mr Chew made no reply except another apeman grunt, which may have been directed at the weeds, not at David. "Fine weather for the Test, isn't it?" said David. He got another grunt. "Are you interestd in cricket, Mr Chew?" he asked, rather desperate by now.

Mr Chew actually spoke. He said "No," heavily, like a lump of earth falling.

"Then I'll explain it to you," David said. "You play with eleven men a side on a pitch twenty-two yards—" Mr Chew turned his head and looked at David. David jumped. Mr Chew was not Chinese. He had huge wiry eyebrows and high cheekbones at the top of great brown slabs of cheek. His mouth was like a cut in the slab and his chin jutted. His nose was a fierce beak. His eyes were very small, very dark, very piercing, and somehow quite savage. David would not have been surprised if Mr Chew had got to his feet and torn him limb from limb. He was sure Mr Chew could have done it very easily too. "The wicket, you know," he said, trying to keep to the subject.

"You," said Mr Chew, fixing his savage eyes on David's. "What's your name?"

"David, sir," said David. The "sir" came quite unintentionally.

Mr Chew thought for a while and inspected David

while he thought. "I'll need to speak to you," he said at length.

"Yes," said David. "I was wanting to talk to you too. About cricket," he went on bravely. "I'd like to tell you how I took five wickets against Radley House last—"

Mr Chew cut short this babbling ruthlessly. "Wait," he said.

"All right." David stood and watched Mr Chew snatch and tear at a weed, and then at another. There is not much you can do if the other person refuses to talk or to listen. Thinking that at least the weeding was keeping Mr Chew away from Luke, David slid his arm down along his leg and took a glance at his watch. As far as he could see, he was lucky if he had been standing beside Mr Chew for two minutes. Even Luke could not deal with Aunt Dot in two minutes.

Mr Chew moved on to another weed, and David noticed an alarming thing. Every time Mr Chew snatched and tore at a weed, it took him down the flowerbed, nearer to the house. Luke had said Mr Chew was stupid, but David began to think that this was because Luke did not go by the usual rules. He suspected that Mr Chew's stupidity might be what most people would call deep cunning. He did his best to halt Mr Chew's progress.

"Er – Mr Chew," he said.

"Wait," said Mr Chew.

David waited, because he could not see what else to do. Together, they moved remorselessly towards the house. And surprisingly quickly. By the time they reached it and David took another look at his watch, only four more minutes had gone by. David saw that the only thing to hope for was that Aunt Dot had thrown Luke out of the house on the spot.

When they were by the wall of the house, Mr Chew stood up. David backed away a step without being able to help it. Mr Chew was not tall, but he loomed. He would have made six of David. He stood looking up and down the wall of the house in a way David did not like at all, and at length he pointed.

"That window," he said. "Whose is that?"

David looked up along Mr Chew's great pointing arm. It was like looking along an oak tree. He could see perfectly well which window Mr Chew meant, but he now had an opportunity to waste time and he took it.

"Which window do you mean? The one at the top is an attic. The next one along is—"

"Third window up," said Mr Chew.

"Oh, *that* one," said David. "You mean that one. That one—" Mr Chew turned and looked at him, savagely. "Mine," said David.

"Underneath it," said Mr Chew, pointing a little lower. "What's that?"

"You mean the creeper?" David said.

"Yes," said Mr Chew. "And there's something wrong with it, isn't there?"

"I see what you mean," said David. "Yes." The creeper was probably dead. Its leaves were brown and curled and singed-looking. Any gardener would have noticed it. But David was fairly sure Mr Chew was not remarking on it because he was a gardener – though what else he was David could not have said.

"That plant," said Mr Chew, "has been burnt. Hasn't it? You tell me how."

"I don't know," David said. After all, he thought, he did not know why it should be burnt just because Luke had climbed up it.

"You don't know?" said Mr Chew.

"No," said David.

"I'll talk to you again later," said Mr Chew, "and maybe you'll remember why by then."

"I don't think so," said David. "I don't know."

"You'll remember," Mr Chew said. He said it slowly, and each word fell out like a heavy, menacing clod of earth. "You'd better remember."

David backed gently away. He was rather frightened of Mr Chew; but on the other hand, he was quite used to people threatening him and trying to make him say and do things he did not want to. He found threats even easier to ignore than guilt. "I'll see you later then," he said.

"You will," Mr Chew promised.

David wandered away round the house. Eight minutes had passed. If Luke were not out of the house by now, there was nothing to be done. Mr Chew had clearly decided that the interview was over and to go on hanging round him was just asking for trouble. David went out of the gate and down the road, wondering how he could find out where Luke was by now, and looked hopefully over gates into gardens as he went, in case Luke was hiding in one of them. He looked over the gate that used to be the Clarksons' and found himself staring into the face of an old gentleman who was spraying roses there.

"Good morning to you," said the old gentleman. "And who might you be? Do you live near here?"

David explained who he was and where he lived.

"Ah," said the old gentleman. "And I am Mr Fry. How do you do?" He proved to be the most courteous and chatty of old gentlemen -- the kind of person Luke could have dealt with beautifully. David stood on one leg, then on the other, and picked loose paint off the gatepost, while Mr Fry told him that he had almost completed his collection of the people who lived in the road, and that David and his relations were the last people he had not met. He wanted to know all about Aunt Dot and Uncle Bernard, and what work Cousin Ronald did. David had never seen Cousin Ronald work, so he could not tell Mr

Fry. Then Mr Fry made him promise to tell Uncle Bernard that he and Mrs Fry would call in one day that week. And at last he let David go.

David shot round the corner into the main road. Luke, no doubt as a disguise, was standing among a line of people at the bus stop. He fell into step beside David as David passed.

"What happened?" they both said at the same time. Then of course they both laughed.

"I got away fairly quickly," Luke said. "I told your Aunt Dot I had to go home for breakfast. But I thought you were never coming. What happened?"

David told him. "And I don't think Mr Chew is stupid," he said.

"Yes he is," said Luke. "Anyone else would have seen it was no good trying to frighten you."

David was highly gratified. "I was frightened," he admitted.

"What if you were?" said Luke. "It wouldn't make you say anything important. The way to get *you* talking is to be friendly – and I just hope none of them realise that." He frowned down at the pavement in a worried way. "David," he said, "I shouldn't keep asking you to do things – it ought to be the other way round – but could you promise not to tell anyone, *anyone* about me? Really about me, I mean."

"Of course," David said. He hoped Luke would go on and explain why, but Luke simply looked at the pavement with his forehead all wrinkled and said nothing. David tried to encourage him by making a joke. "Funny," he said, "that Mr Chew turned up on Chewsday."

"Funnier still if he'd turned up on Monday," Luke said. He seemed to have missed the point, which was unlike him. But he was obviously thinking of something else. "I have been a fool!" he said. "I was too glad to be out to think – if you knew what it was like down there, you'd have been glad too. I should have realised they'd track me down – but they knew when the lock was broken, if I'd only thought – and I ought to have guessed I wouldn't have quite the old control at first. But, no, I have to go and burn that creeper. Then I get really stupid and make that fire yesterday. They knew that was me all right. And to crown it all, I have to go to sleep on the end of your bed and let Chew catch up with me. I must be getting old, or something."

"You don't seem old to me," David said.

"I never *seem* old to anyone," said Luke. "But I must be, or I wouldn't have been so tired. I expect it's being shut up for so long."

"How long were you shut up?" David asked curiously.

Luke took a sudden fierce turn to cheerfulness. "Oh, I've lost count."

David tried another question. "And who is Mr Chew?"

"Distant relative," Luke said merrily. "About the same as your Cousin Ronald is to you."

David saw that Luke had somehow talked himself into a more carefree state of mind. In a way he was glad, but he was also a little sorry, because he knew Luke was not going to tell him any more. "So what are you going to do?" he asked.

Sure enough, Luke smiled in the way that meant he was not telling. "I'll manage. As long as you keep your mouth shut and don't meet me in the house again. Now, what shall we do?"

"Play cricket," said David.

VII FLOWERS

David and Luke spent an excellent morning playing cricket in the recreation ground. There, they met a plump and placid boy called Alan, who was only too glad to let them play in his team. This team was losing when David and Luke joined it. A very few overs from David put a stop to that.

"I say! You're a good bowler, aren't you!" Alan said admiringly, as the fourth wicket fell.

David grinned, and was much inclined to like Alan. He hoped Luke liked him too. But, to his surprise, Luke hardly seemed aware that Alan existed. When Luke spoke, it was to David, and, for all the notice he took of Alan or any of the other boys, they might not have been playing at all. David was rather irritated.

"I like Alan," he said, when the game finished. "Don't you?"

"Who's Alan?" Luke said vaguely. Then he seemed to remember. "Oh – I suppose he's all right," he said.

David, as he walked home through Ashbury, wondered if this was another example of Luke's strangeness. But it could equally well have been because Luke was so worried about Mr Chew. Beside Mr Chew, Alan or anyone else did seem rather unimportant.

Trouble began again when David, clean, changed and tidy, came in to lunch.

"Ah, David," said Aunt Dot. "Why did you not tell me you had met that charming and nicely-spoken child who was here this morning? What is his name?"

"Luke," said Astrid, raising her eyebrows at David.

"Yes, Luke," said Aunt Dot. "He tells me he lives with Mr and Mrs Fry at the end of the road. At least," she corrected herself, because she was always very strict about facts, "I asked if he did and he said Yes."

David wondered how Luke was ever going to keep up this piece of dishonesty. Would it be possible to persuade courteous old Mr Fry to join in? David rather thought not. "I met Mr Fry this morning," he said, hoping Aunt Dot would see it as supporting evidence. "He said they were going to call on you, him and Mrs Fry."

Uncle Bernard at once went frail. "My dear Dot, I can't meet these people. Not at my time of life."

"Nonsense, Bernard," said Aunt Dot. "David, I think it very impolite of you not to have introduced Luke to us before this."

David sighed. Aunt Dot always contrived to blame him about something, even when she was pleased. "I only met him on Sunday," he explained.

"Then you should have introduced him at *once*," said Aunt Dot. "As he is exactly the companion I would have chosen for you, I want you to bring him here this afternoon."

David knew this was out of the question, because of Mr Chew. So he was forced into a piece of dishonesty of his own. "Luke can't come out this afternoon. His cousin's come – on a visit, you know."

"Then bring him tomorrow," said Aunt Dot.

David was heartily relieved when lunch was over. He had arranged to meet Luke in the recreation ground, so, as soon as he had changed, he left the house and scudded down the front drive to the gate. He got a very nasty shock when Mr Chew stood up from behind a wheelbarrow and took hold of his arm.

Mr Chew was quite as strong as he looked. David

tugged mightily to get his arm away, but Mr Chew's great arm did not even tremble. The horny fingers simply closed a trifle.

"And where were you going?" said Mr Chew.

"Nowhere," said David. "Let go."

"Going to meet someone," said Mr Chew. "Perhaps I'll come too."

"I'm not going to meet anyone. Let go. I'm only – I've only come out because my Aunt wanted me to pick some flowers," David lied. After all, Mr Chew was not to know he was forbidden to touch flowers.

Mr Chew let go of David's arm and, putting his great hands on his hips, backed round until he was between David and the gate. "Go on," he said. "Let's see you."

David rubbed his arm and saw that he was not going to get past Mr Chew in a hurry. He would have to wait. He turned to go back into the house.

"Oh no," said Mr Chew. "Come back. Pick flowers. Let's see you."

David turned round, and was suddenly filled with black rage against Mr Chew. "All right," he said. "I'll pick flowers. So there!"

And under Mr Chew's sarcastic eye, he picked flowers, right and left, all down each side of the path. He was too angry to care. When he had a big bunch of Cousin Ronald's geraniums, he thrust them towards Mr Chew's beaked nose.

"There," he said. "Flowers. Smell."

"Beautiful," said Mr Chew, without turning a hair.

David swung round and stalked back into the house with the bunch of geraniums, knowing that, in his relations' eyes, he could not have been more of a criminal if each flower had been a dead body. Like a murderer trying to cover his crime, he crept upstairs with them and into the best spare bedroom, where he remembered there was a very ugly jug. He filled it with water, stuffed the flowers in it, and spread them out a bit. They did not look very nice. Then, deciding that the place where they were least likely to be noticed was somewhere where there often were flowers, he tiptoed past Aunt Dot's room and arranged them on the landing window-sill. Then he fled guiltily to his own room.

And there he was forced to stay. Every time he tried to get out of the house, Mr Chew was there, whether he tried at the front, the side or the back. David gave up in the end and crossly read a book.

The flowers were discovered during supper. Cousin Ronald was busy boring everyone about what an excellent gardener Mr Chew was, with slightly more interesting digressions on why England drew with Australia in the Test, when Mrs Thirsk came in, carrying the ugly jug.

"I think you ought to see this," she said.

David drew a deep angry breath and thought he might have known it would be Mrs Thirsk who found out.

"My Worcester!" said Aunt Dot.

"My Geraniums!" said Cousin Ronald.

"David!" said Uncle Bernard vigorously.

"They were on the landing window-sill," explained righteous Mrs Thirsk.

"I think that was a very nice thought," Astrid said unexpectedly. The rest, David included, stared at her in astonishment. Astrid went rather red. "Flowers are always a nice thought," she said.

"It was pure disobedience," said Cousin Ronald.

"I'm sure David was only trying to please," said Astrid. "There's never any pleasing you, Ronald. Can't you tell a nice thought when you see one?"

"My geraniums are not a nice thought," said Cousin Ronald. "And that jug is valuable."

"You can go to bed, boy," said Uncle Bernard. "Here and now."

"Without supper?" David said, truly dismayed.

"Exactly," said Aunt Dot.

David got up to go. But he did not see why Mr Chew should get away with his bullying. "Mr Chew told me to pick them," he said.

"None of your lies," said Cousin Ronald. "Chew is an excellent fellow."

"If you ask me, he's more like the Abominable Snowman," said Astrid.

"We were not asking you," said Uncle Bernard. "Leave the room, David."

David trailed to the door, past triumphant Mrs Thirsk. Behind him, Astrid said: "You deprive him of supper just because of a bunch of flowers! To hear you, you'd think geraniums were more important than people!"

As David walked upstairs, there was a clamour of voices in the dining-room, suggesting that everyone, down to Mrs Thirsk, had turned on Astrid. David had known them do that before from time to time. He trailed to his room. Mr Chew was still gardening away outside, so there was no possibility of fetching Luke for company. David began a long barren evening – no Luke, no doodles, no supper.

Almost no supper. Two hours or so later, someone thumped on the door. David answered it with a forsaken mutter and hoped they would go away. To his surprise, Astrid put her head round the door, looking rather white and red round the eyes. "Here," she said. "I can't see you go hungry. Catch!"

David caught – in the slips it would have counted as a very good catch – a large packet of biscuits. "Thanks," he said.

"Don't mench," said Astrid. "I can't stay. Dot says to

68

remind you to bring Luke tomorrow." Before David could tell her this was impossible, Astrid had gone.

When your bed is full of biscuit crumbs, you wake early. David woke very early, among crumbs, sunshine and birdsong, and went at once to the window in hopes that Mr Chew had not yet arrived.

Mr Chew was there. He was standing in the middle of the dewy lawn, talking to another man. David, as Luke had done the day before, got himself away from the centre of the window at once and looked at them round the edge of the curtain. The other man had his back to the house, and what David could see of him looked ordinary and respectable enough. He was taller than Mr Chew and nothing like so wide, and he was wearing the kind of dark suit that Cousin Ronald's friends usually wore. But Cousin Ronald's friends did not usually walk in the dew with Mr Chew.

Mr Chew was doing most of the talking. David saw him wave one great arm up the garden and suspected he was telling the other man about the rebuilt wall. Then, after more gestures, he swung round and pointed at the house, straight at David's window. The stranger turned to look. David saw nothing of what followed, because he was pressed against the wall beside the window hoping he had not been seen. When he dared to look again, the stranger had gone. Mr Chew was digging viciously at a rose bed, and the only living things near him were some big black birds watching the spade for worms.

"You think you've got me, don't you?" David said to the distant Mr Chew. "Well, you're wrong. You've not got me, and you've not got Luke either. I'll get out this morning. You'll see."

A vow like this is easy to make but not so easy to fulfil. For what seemed ages, David hung about after breakfast, waiting for Mr Chew's attention to be fixed elsewhere, but, at the same time, he did not dare let Aunt Dot see him, because he was in his jeans, now very grubby and comfortable indeed. Aunt Dot was anxious to see him. David heard her say several times: "Where *is* David? I want him to bring his friend here."

"I did remind him, Dot," Astrid said.

"It is not merely reminding David needs," Aunt Dot replied. "If he is to remember a thing, it must be dinned in his ears."

David had several narrow escapes while Aunt Dot irritably searched for him. But at last what he had been hoping for happened. Cousin Ronald marched masterfully up the garden to tell Mr Chew how to spray roses. Mr Chew pushed his dirty hat back, scratched his wiry hair, and gave Cousin Ronald his attention. David pelted for the front door.

"David!" said Aunt Dot from the rear.

This is the kind of summons you ignore. David slammed the front door, shot down the drive and was out of the gate before the echoes from the door had died away. Down the road he went, a hurried jog-trot, with the matches rattling on his hip, wondering where it would be safe to strike one and fetch Luke. Courteous old Mr Fry had caught someone else that morning. He was waving his rose-spray earnestly while he talked to a man in a dark suit, who was leaning with one hand on Mr Fry's gate, nodding and smiling pleasantly at Mr Fry.

Something about the shape of that dark suit caused David's steps to slow, then to halt altogether. It could have been the man who was talking to Mr Chew. Not quite sure, David stood still, about a wicket-length away.

Mr Fry saw him and waved the rose-spray. "Good morning, my young friend!"

The man leaning on the gate turned, casually and

pleasantly, to see who Mr Fry was calling to. His face was perfectly pleasant. But David's stomach pitched about, because the way he turned was the same as the way he had turned when Mr Chew pointed to David's window.

"Morning," David called to Mr Fry. Then, with his hands in his pockets, he turned and sauntered back the way he had come. He tried to look casual and carefree, but he was seething with frustration and rather frightened too. The road was a dead-end. The only way out was past Mr Fry's house, and the stranger was posted there. No wonder Mr Chew could afford to give Cousin Ronald his attention.

Miserably, David went back into the house and pulled the door shut. Miserably, he trudged up to his room and sat on his bed, wondering how he was to get out of the house and warn Luke there were now two people after him. He simply could not see how to do it.

As he sat there, he heard voices downstairs. He could tell that Aunt Dot was still looking for him to make him fetch Luke. Fetch Luke! It was just like Aunt Dot to make things really difficult. The best thing was to stay quiet and hope she gave up.

But a minute later, hurried feet pounded on the stairs. Someone gave a hasty bang at his door and burst in. It was Astrid.

"Oh, there you are!" she said. "Thank goodness! Quick, get into those good clothes, or Dot'll eat us both, and then make haste to the drawing-room. You're wanted."

"All right." Sighing, David stood up.

"Hurry!" said Astrid. "She'll come herself in a minute!"

David hurried, feeling that this was all he needed to make this the worst day of the holiday. Three minutes later, he was ready and Astrid was rapidly brushing his hair, with hard prickly swipes. "There," she said. "Now run."

"Drawing-room?" David asked, puzzled. It was a big stiffly-furnished room in the front of the house where he was very seldom allowed to go.

"Yes," said Astrid. "And run."

David did not exactly see the need to run, but he went fairly swiftly downstairs and quite briskly into the drawing-room. There he stopped as if he had walked into a wall. The stranger in the dark suit turned towards him with a pleasant smile. He was standing in the middle of the room, quite at his ease. Around him, Aunt Dot, Uncle Bernard and Cousin Ronald did not look at ease at all. Cousin Ronald looked almost ill, yellow and pinched and much more like Uncle Bernard than usual.

"Good morning, David," said the stranger pleasantly.

"David," said Cousin Ronald, "this is Mr Wedding. He has come to take you out to lunch."

VIII MR WEDDING

"How do you do?" David said hopelessly.

Mr Wedding held out his hand. "I hope," he said, as David took hold of it, "you'll give me the pleasure of your company. Your guardians have agreed."

David tried to muster the rather large amount of courage it was going to take to refuse. To help muster it, he looked up into Mr Wedding's face. He was thoroughly taken aback to find that, close to, it was the kind of face he could not help liking. It was an agreeable, firm face, not young and not old, and rather lined. These lines, combined with a strange, searching way Mr Wedding had of looking, made David feel he would like to get to know Mr Wedding – although he also had a feeling that it would be rather difficult to do so.

"I do advise you to come," Mr Wedding said. He said it amiably, even laughingly, but there was a good hint of warning to it too. He was letting David know that there was going to be trouble if he refused, because Mr Wedding had somehow got David's relations on his side. But the most perplexing thing was the way David found himself wanting to go with Mr Wedding, and very pleased to be asked. He struggled for a moment, and then found he had to give in.

"Thanks," he said. "I'd love to come."

His relations began telling him he was to mind his manners and remember to thank Mr Wedding afterwards. While they talked, David bit his tongue hard and told himself that this Mr Wedding was certainly an enemy of Luke's and he must be careful what he said to him.

Mr Wedding's car was waiting outside the front gate. It was big, white and expensive, with a lady chauffeur at the wheel. She smiled at David as Mr Wedding opened the rear door for him to get in, and David smiled back. She was one of the prettiest ladies he had ever seen.

"I think we'll go out to Wallsey," Mr Wedding said to her. "That suit you?" he asked David.

"I think so," said David. "At least, I've never been." He had heard of the place, of course, but he had no real idea where it was or what it was like.

"Wallsey," said Mr Wedding, and got in beside David.

The way to Wallsey seemed to be through the centre of Ashbury. Before long, David saw Trubitt's and, on the other side of the street, the black-windowed shell of the burnt building. He could not resist craning his head round to have another look at the damage. When he turned back, he found Mr Wedding watching him. David felt his face going scarlet, because he had let Mr Wedding see he was interested in the building; but some of his shame was the way he had caused so much damage simply by a careless word to Luke. He was afraid Mr Wedding was going to ask him about it, but Mr Wedding said nothing. They drove out of Ashbury.

"You know," said Mr Wedding at last, "I really know next to nothing about you, David. Could you tell me about yourself?"

David sensed danger. "I – I don't think there's anything to tell," he said.

"School?" suggested Mr Wedding. "You go away to school?"

This was harmless enough, and nothing to do with Luke. David admitted he went away to school. But Mr Wedding seemed interested. He asked so many questions and understood David's answers so readily, that before long David was telling him all about the French master everyone thought was mad, friends, enemies, food, cricket; the time the whole class made groaning-noises behind old Didgett's back, books, cricket; the day he and Kent got locked in the pavilion, cricket; the punch-up with 3B, and cricket again. It was a long way to Wallsey. David had plenty of time to tell Mr Wedding how he had taken five wickets against Radley House, and, because Mr Wedding evidently appreciated his cunning, he described the ball which had defeated each batsman: off-break, leg-break, and the quicker one that got in under the bat and uprooted the middle stump.

While he was describing the fifth wicket, which had really been something of an accident, David noticed that the countryside he could see from the windows of the car was strange and wild. There were steep hills, very green grass, and waterfalls dashing down past pine-trees. It reminded him a little of Norway, or the Lakes. He turned to ask Mr Wedding where they were.

Before he could ask, Mr Wedding said: "We're nearly there now. Look."

There was a wide, misty lake ahead, and a green island in the lake. A long arching bridge led from the land to the island, held up by a spider-web of girders. As the car rumbled up the arch, the sun shone in through the bright ironwork, breaking up into hundreds of rainbow colours which half dazzled David. He was still blinking when the car stopped and they got out at what seemed to be an inn. The lady drove the car away, and Mr Wedding led David to a table outside in the sun, where there was a view over the misty lake to the brown hills beyond it.

"What would you like to drink?" said Mr Wedding.

"Milk-shake, please," said David.

The barman brought it at once, and beer for Mr Wedding. Mr Wedding sat down at the table and stretched, as if he found it pleasant to relax, and David sat down opposite him feeling anything but relaxed. This must be where Mr Wedding got down to business.

But no. "I don't much care for those people you live with," said Mr Wedding. "Do you?"

While he was speaking, David tasted the milk-shake. It left him little attention for anything else. Never had he tasted anything so marvellous. He wondered how Mr Wedding could prefer beer. "No," he said. "No, I don't like them either."

"But you have to live with them?" said Mr Wedding.

"Yes," said David. "When they don't send me off somewhere. And," he continued bitterly – and whether it was the effect of the milk-shake, or the strange clear air on the lake, or the fact that he now seemed to know Mr Wedding so well that made him say it, he did not know – "and I'm supposed to be *grateful*. I wouldn't mind them nagging so much, or being boring, or forbidding things, or going on about manners and sending me to bed without supper all the time, if only I didn't have to be grateful all the time. I am grateful. They do look after me all right. But I wish I didn't have to be."

Mr Wedding thought about this, drumming his fingers on his beer-mug. "I'm not sure you do have to be grateful," he said at last.

David looked up from the milk-shake in astonishment. "You're joking," he said doubtfully.

Mr Wedding shook his head. "No. I'm quite in earnest. Look at it this way. You're still a child, and you can't earn your living or look after yourself properly. When you were younger, you could do it even less. All children are the same. So the law says that someone has to look after you until you can do it for yourself – your guardians in your case. And there's another law which says that when you drop a stone it falls to the ground. Are you grateful to that stone for falling, or does the stone ask the earth to be grateful?"

"I – oh —" David felt there was something missing from this. "But people aren't stones."

"Of course not. And if people do anything over and above the law, then you can be grateful if you want. But no one should ask it of you."

"I see," said David. "Yes. Thanks." As he sucked the last bubbles of the milk-shake loudly up the straw, he thought about what Mr Wedding had said, and it was like having a huge weight slowly levered off his back. He felt lighter and lighter, and happier and happier. "Thank you, Mr Wedding."

"If you've finished that stuff," said Mr Wedding, "you might come and look at the river."

The river thundered over green rocks just beyond the inn, wonderfully clear, with the sun making moving circles on the stones at the bottom. David only waited to ask before he had his shoes and socks off and his prickly trousers rolled up and had bounded into the cool water. It ran so briskly that it stood up in fans beside his legs. There were shells on the bottom of a kind he had never seen before, and stones like round jewels. Blissfully, David waded, threw stones, collected others and picked up shells, until Mr Wedding strolled down the bank and said it was time for lunch. David put his collection of shells and stones in his pocket and his socks and shoes back on, and they went back to the inn. There they had the most magnificent food David had ever eaten. He ate so much that he had to sit rather carefully afterwards.

Finally, Mr Wedding pushed his chair back and looked at David in a way that was different and difficult. David abruptly forgot that he had overeaten.

"David," said Mr Wedding, "I'm very anxious to find someone whom I imagine goes by the name of Luke. Can you help me at all?"

"No," said David. "I'm sorry, Mr Wedding. I can't."

"Perhaps you mean you won't?" suggested Mr Wedding.

"Yes, but I still can't," David said.

"But there must be one or two things you can tell me," Mr Wedding said thoughtfully. "For instance, how you came to let Luke out. I thought I was the only one who knew how to do that."

"I did it by accident, trying to curse," said David.

Mr Wedding laughed. He threw back his head and laughed very heartily, but David, all the same, had a notion that Mr Wedding was not amused – or not quite in the way he or Luke were when they laughed. "You did it by accident!" he said. "I wish I believed in accidents. Where is Luke now?"

"I don't know," David said truthfully.

"But you can find him when you want to?" said Mr Wedding.

Before David had decided what to say to that, a swirl of black pinions was beating the sky over his head. He ducked and put one arm up, but the creature passed him and landed with a heavy *clack* on the table beside Mr Wedding's coffee cup. It was a great black crow. "That gave me a shock!" he said. The crow glanced at him over its shoulder and then looked up at Mr Wedding.

It said something. David knew it said something, though he could not catch the words.

"It talks," he said, fascinated.

"Just a moment," said Mr Wedding. "Where?"

The crow said something else.

"I see," said Mr Wedding. "That's no good then. I'll tell you what to do later."

"Is it a crow?" asked David. "Will it talk to me?"

"A raven," said Mr Wedding. "And I doubt if it will talk to you, but you can try if you like."

"Er – raven," said David. "Hallo." Cautiously he stretched a finger out to the bird's large shiny back and gently touched its warm, stiff feathers. "Will you talk to me too?"

The raven turned one eye on him. David could not help thinking it looked rather an evil creature. It put him in mind of a vulture. "Yes, I'll talk to you if you want," it said, and David could not stop himself grinning with pride. He could see that Mr Wedding was really surprised. The bird hunched up to scratch the top of its head with its big grey foot, and looked at David from under its leg. "I saw Luke just now," it remarked. "He was trying to find you."

"Don't tell me where he was, then," David said.

"It won't matter. He saw me and went away," said the raven. "We've lost him for the moment."

"Good," said David.

"Hm," said Mr Wedding. "I think that will do. Off you go."

"Going," said the bird and took off with its legs trailing, in another great black sweep of feathers. Looking up, David saw it circling with its wing-pinions spread like fingers while it came round into the wind and tucked up its grey feet like an aeroplane retracting its undercarriage. "I'll see you," it called. Then it was away across the lake with large leisurely flaps of its wings.

"Brilliant!" said David, watching it get slowly smaller against the hills.

"They don't often talk to anyone but me," Mr Wedding said. "You were lucky – I suppose lucky is the word for it. May I speak to you seriously, David?"

"Yes," said David, a little apprehensively. "What?"

79

"You don't know much about me, do you?" said Mr Wedding.

David looked up at him to agree, and to protest a little. And he saw Mr Wedding had only one eye. David stared. For a moment, he was more frightened than he had ever been in his life. He could not understand it. Up till then, there had been nothing strange about Mr Wedding's face at all, and it had been perfectly ordinary. David had not noticed a change. Yet one of Mr Wedding's eyes was simply not there. The place where the second eye should have been had an eyelid and eyelashes, so that it looked almost as if Mr Wedding had shut one eye – but not quite. It did not look at all horrible. There was no reason to be frightened. But David was. Mr Wedding's remaining eye had something to do with it. It made up for the other by gazing so piercingly blue, so deep and difficult, that it was as wild and strange in its way as Mr Chew's face. As David looked from eye to empty eyelid and back, he had suddenly no doubt that what he was seeing was Mr Wedding's true face, and his real nature. The hair on David's spine stood up, slowly and nastily, as he looked.

"And I suspect you don't know much about Luke," Mr Wedding went on. "He was not shut up without very good reason, you know. Would it surprise you to hear that he did something very terrible indeed?"

David, thankful to think of something beside Mr Wedding's one eye, thought of Luke making the fire, and the hair on his back uncomfortably laid itself down again while he did so. "No, it wouldn't surprise me," he said. He knew Luke well enough now to see the way he would have done the terrible thing – with a strange, absent-minded smile, because whatever it was had been a clever idea and rather difficult to do. "Luke doesn't work by the usual rules," he explained. "And I don't think you do, either," he said, struck by a strange similarity between Mr Wedding and Luke which he could not quite pin down.

Mr Wedding smiled a little. "You're right," he said. "I don't. But there are rules for everyone all the same, and Luke broke them. He went on breaking them even when he was shut up. He took a revenge on us from prison which has had serious consequences already and is going to have worse. I'm not asking you simply to hand him over to justice, David. I must ask him about what he did. Now will you help me?"

This seemed a very reasonable appeal. David thought. "What revenge did he take?"

"I can't tell you that. You'll just have to take my word that it was serious."

David thought again, and he thought that he probably did not blame Luke for taking a revenge. If Luke really had been in prison – and now that Mr Wedding said so, it seemed that it must be true – then David had no doubt that it had been horrible. Remembering Luke's face when he first saw Mr Chew was enough. And, after all, David had tried to curse his own relatives at the mere idea of being shut up for the holidays with Mr Scrum.

"I could help you," he said, "but only if you swear not to shut Luke up again." Mr Wedding drew in a breath, and David added hurriedly: "Or punish him any other way."

Mr Wedding let his breath out again in a sigh. "No," he said. "That I can't promise."

"Then I can't help you," said David.

"Then I'll tell you something," said Mr Wedding, with his one blue eye most piercingly on David. "I don't think you've noticed that this place where we are now is somewhere where nobody could ever find you." David took a puzzled look at the inn and round at the lake and the mountains. "Yes, it's Wallsey all right," said Mr Wedding, "but that's not where you think it is. If it came to it, I could keep you here and make things very unpleasant for you until you tell me how to find Luke. Remember I don't work by the usual rules either. Now what do you say?"

David took hold of the table rather hard and the hair on his spine pricked up again. He had no doubt that Mr Wedding could make things very unpleasant indeed. On the other hand, so could Uncle Bernard and Aunt Dot, and it would make a change from them. "No, I can't tell you," he said.

"Doesn't the idea frighten you at all?" Mr Wedding asked, seeming rather interested.

"Yes it does," David admitted. "But I don't want to tell you about Luke."

Mr Wedding sat back, rather thoughtfully. "I see why Chew got nowhere," he said. "All right, forget that. Suppose I were to give you something you very much want for telling me?"

"Such as?" asked David. He had a moment when he thought wistfully of a dog.

"Such as arranging for you not to live with those guardians of yours any more," said Mr Wedding.

"Oh, could you do that?" David said eagerly.

"Very easily," said Mr Wedding.

This was temptation indeed. Golden thoughts of living entirely alone – except for a dog – came into David's head. Beautiful peace without Aunt Dot or Uncle Bernard or – but David knew this was nothing but a daydream. Mr Wedding himself had said that children had to live with someone, and, as Cousin Ronald had several times pointed out, if his relations had not taken David in, he would have been sent to live in an orphanage. And, whatever an orphanage was like, you were not alone in it. "No," David said sadly. "Sorry, Mr Wedding."

"Please don't apologise," Mr Wedding said courteously. "After all, there's no apology possible for such extreme rudeness." David thought he was joking at first and looked up, ready to laugh. But Mr Wedding was obviously displeased and had gone most unfriendly. "I suppose you don't understand," he said, rather disgustedly, "and the laws of hospitality mean nothing to you. I've given you some advice which you might have gone through all your life without learning anywhere else, and I've given you a good meal. In return, you treat me as an enemy. You don't appear to understand that the least you can do is to help me find Luke."

"Oh no I needn't," said David.

"How do you make that out?" Mr Wedding asked scornfully.

"I haven't lived with Uncle Bernard all these years without knowing when someone isn't playing fair," said David. "I've had a marvellous time and a brilliant lunch – and thank you – and the advice was better still. But you can't tell me that the earth's not grateful to a stone for being dropped on and then say I owe you for lunch. You did it all for a reason and that's not fair."

To David's great relief, Mr Wedding burst out laughing. "Well done!" he said. "My own weapons turned against me. All right, you win, David." Still laughing, he pushed back his chair and stood up. At once, as if he had given a signal, the big white car came gliding round the corner and stopped in front of them, ready to take David home.

The pretty lady got out and held the rear door open for David. Although David was extremely glad that he seemed to have come through without giving Luke away, he could not help looking regretfully up at the green hill above the inn and down at the misty, rippling lake. The weather was quite hot enough for swimming. But David knew he could hardly ask Mr Wedding to let him stay. He sighed and went to the car.

IX THE RAVEN

"Oh, just a moment!" said Mr Wedding. David turned round. "Your relations," said Mr Wedding. "They'll probably want to know what I said to you, and I don't think they'll understand a word of the truth. Shall we say that I'm one of your teachers?"

David chuckled. "All right."

Mr Wedding took hold of the car door and nodded to the lady, who went back to the driving-seat. Then he nodded to David and David started to get into the car. "By the way," said Mr Wedding. David took his head out of the car again. "I ought not to let you go away with those shells and stones in your pocket, really," Mr Wedding said. "But, as you've done so well, you can keep them."

"Thanks," said David. "Aren't you coming then?"

"Not just now," said Mr Wedding. "But I'll see you again. In you get." David got in and sat down. Mr Wedding had almost closed the door, when he thought of something else. He opened the door and leaned in. "David," he said, "what do you say to a contest over Luke?"

"What sort of contest?" David said cautiously.

"A battle of wits, if you like," said Mr Wedding. "I can see yours are pretty sharp. Suppose we agree that I can do all in my power to find Luke, and you can use every way in your power to stop me. What do you say?"

85

David saw two things wrong with this at once. "You don't work on my rules," he pointed out.

Mr Wedding drummed his fingers on the car roof and thought. "Yes, but you haven't mobilised half your resources yet, have you? You can do anything you like to stop me."

"All right," said David. All sorts of cunning plans came jostling into his head, and he smiled happily. But he did not forget his second objection. "You have to have a time limit. You have to say that if I can keep Luke safe till the end of the holidays, then you'll stop looking for him and won't punish him or hurt him if you find him after that."

"Agreed," said Mr Wedding. "But let's not make it so long. Let's say that if you can keep Luke safe until next Sunday, then he's safe for good. All right?"

This shook David a little. Mr Wedding must be very sure of winning to set such a short limit. But he felt he had agreed to too much already to refuse a detail like that. "All right," he said.

"Splendid," said Mr Wedding, and he shut the car door and stood back.

The journey back seemed much shorter. Hardly had they rumbled over the iron bridge than they were in the outskirts of Ashbury, and thence it was no more than five minutes before they were in Lockend and turning into the road, past Mr Fry's house. The car stopped outside Uncle Bernard's house, and the lady got out and opened the door before David could get to it. As David passed her, she held out her right hand.

"Shake," she said. David shook hands, rather shyly. "Good luck," she said. "But you won't do it, you know."

"Want to bet?" said David.

The lady laughed and shook her head. "No. It wouldn't be fair."

If anything more was needed to make David determined that Mr Wedding should not win, this was it. He ground his teeth together as he went up the drive, and swore to keep Luke safe if it killed him.

Indoors, everyone was having tea in the drawing-room. David knew they had been waiting for him, because as he shut the front door, Uncle Bernard called out: "Come in here, boy."

As David went reluctantly into the room, he looked at them all in the light of Mr Wedding's advice. They all seemed exactly the same. Uncle Bernard was yellow and withered and propped on six silk cushions, claiming to have lumbago. Aunt Dot was pouring tea like a good-mannered robot made of some very hard grey metal, and Cousin Ronald was eating cakes with his usual gusto. Astrid was propped on two silk cushions and seemed discontented, just as usual.

"Well?" said Uncle Bernard. "There's no need to confess that you forgot to say thank you. I know you did."

"I didn't forget," said David. "I—"

Cousin Ronald interrupted, eagerly and nervously. "What did he say to you? What did you talk about?"

"School for a lot of the time," David said. "He's one of the masters, you know. The – er – the – General Studies."

Cousin Ronald's face went bright shiny pink. "Thank Heaven for that! I thought he was—"

"I'm sure David does not want to know what you thought," said Aunt Dot. "David, I think it would be a very nice idea if you were to go and ask your friend Luke to come and have tea with us."

"Thanks," said David. "Now?" He could not help smiling, because one of his cunning ideas had been to get Aunt Dot to be a kind of guard on Luke. No one, in David's experience, ever got the better of Aunt Dot.

"Now, of course," said Aunt Dot.

David scudded from the room. A glance out of the hall window showed him Mr Chew, digging sullenly near the garden shed. That meant the front garden was free. David slipped out of the front door and down the drive. At the front gate, he stopped and felt among his pocketful of stones and shells for the matches. He had almost taken the box out when his eyes met the one round eye of the raven. It was sitting on the gatepost, very large and smooth and greeny-black. David dropped the box into his pocket and took his hand out empty.

"Oh – hallo," he said awkwardly.

"Hallo," said the bird. "I'd better warn you that I'm supposed to follow you wherever you go."

"Thanks," David said bitterly. "Nice of you to tell me."

"It's only fair to tell you," said the bird. "You don't know all the facts."

"No. But I'm finding out, aren't I?" said David. "Thanks anyway."

"You must ask me anything else you want to know," replied the bird, and it took off, tucking up its grey feet as it rose, and settled on the gable over the best spare room.

David looked up at it miserably. Mr Wedding had mobilised his resources all right – and the one thing he wanted to know he could not ask the raven: how to fetch Luke without its knowing. He was stuck for the moment. There was nothing he could do but loiter beside the gate for about the length of time it took to get to Mr Fry's house and back, and then go indoors again. David loitered, and began to see that the only safe thing he could do – safe for Luke, anyway – was simply not to strike a match until next Monday. But he felt that was a last resort. That made it no battle of wits at all, and, for all David knew, Mr Wedding might have other ways of finding Luke. What he needed to do was to consult Luke, to tell him that Mr Wedding was after him, ask him just what Mr Wedding's resources were, and arrange some kind of plan. Besides, he wanted to see Luke anyway, just as a friend.

"Luke can't come out just now," he told Aunt Dot. "There's another person that wants to see him."

Aunt Dot was displeased. "I shall write to Mr Fry myself," she said. David wondered what would happen when she did. Disaster seemed to be threatening from every quarter. He saw that he would have to talk to Luke soon.

No opportunity offered. Supper was plain pink meat and plain pink blancmange and David did not feel very hungry. As soon as he could, he asked to get down. Aunt Dot had just given him permission, when there was a sudden hullabaloo from the kitchen. Mrs Thirsk was shouting. It sounded as if chairs and saucepans were falling about too.

"What on earth?" said Cousin Ronald, beginning to get up.

Before he could get up properly, or anyone else could move at all, Mr Chew came flying past outside the french window with his gash of a mouth stretched into an unpleasant grin, and after him came Mrs Thirsk, purple in the face, aiming blows at Mr Chew with a rolling-pin and shouting.

"You dirty beast! You bandy-legged old sneak!" screamed Mrs Thirsk, and *thump* went the rolling-pin on Mr Chew's back.

Cousin Ronald stayed just as he was, with his knees bent and one hand on the back of his chair, and stared. Everyone else stared too, while Mr Chew pelted nimbly up the garden on his crooked legs and Mrs Thirsk pounded after him. At the top of the garden, Mr Chew seized a spade which was leaning against the shed and turned at bay with it. Smiling hugely, he seemed to ask Mrs Thirsk to come on and get him.

Mrs Thirsk did. She came on like a maddened bull, and they heard the *crack* of the rolling-pin on Mr Chew's head even in the dining-room. Mr Chew, not turning a hair, swung the spade and smacked Mrs Thirsk on the behind with it. Mrs Thirsk hopped like a dervish, dropped the rolling-pin and seized a garden fork, with which she went for Mr Chew like a gladiator. David gazed at the battle, enchanted. Never had he seen a more beautiful sight. The raven seemed to share his opinion. He saw it swoop down over the red face and jabbing fork of Mrs Thirsk, wheeling and fluttering in the greatest excitement, and then beat about Mr Chew's hat, egging him on to hit harder.

It was too good a chance to miss. Besides, Aunt Dot had pulled herself together and was sailing towards the window to stop the fight. David ran. He ran through the house, down the drive, up the road, and did not stop running until he reached the nearest of the deserted yards he had discovered with Luke. It was full of scrap metal. David swung himself into the cab of a derelict lorry and, without waiting to get his breath back, struck a match. Then, while he got his breath, he turned the match over in his fingers, lovingly preserving the flame, watching the burnt end grow and twist.

Before the flame reached his fingers, Luke swung himself up from the other side of the lorry. He was out of breath too, and flung himself into the cab with such a clatter that he startled a great black crow off a nearby roof.

"Thank goodness!" they both said. And both laughed.

"Phew!" said Luke. "It's Wedding now isn't it? I saw one of his ravens this afternoon. What happened?"

David explained what had happened. Luke, as he told him, kept chuckling in a surprised, appreciative way.

"He did you proud, didn't he?" he said. "He must have taken a fancy to you. But isn't that just like him to jump you into a contest when you thought it was all over! And I must say I wish you hadn't agreed."

"So do I now," said David. "Perhaps the best thing is if I don't strike a match until Monday, and you keep well hidden."

Luke would not hear of it. Like David, he thought it would make a very poor contest. He propped his feet high on the steering wheel of the lorry, folded his arms on his chest and pooh-poohed the idea. "Nonsense," he said. "Wedding may be clever and he may have a great many powers, but he always had to rely on me when it came to real cunning. I rather fancy slipping by under their noses. You just distract that bird and get well away from the house and we'll be all right."

"How do I distract it?" said David. "Arrange for Mrs Thirsk to beat up old Chew every time I want to go out?"

Luke grinned at him past his own knees, since his feet were propped above his head. "Ravens," he said, "are very greedy birds. And another thing – he probably only knows you by your clothes and the colour of your hair. Try fooling him by looking a bit different."

David found it very cheering, the way Luke never seemed daunted by any difficulty. He thought nothing, either, of David's worry about Aunt Dot writing to Mr Fry.

"I can handle your Aunt," he said. "I expect I can deal with this Mr Fry of yours too. Not to worry." Then he became more serious and looked at his uptilted feet rather intently. "What did Wedding say about this revenge I'm supposed to have taken?"

"Nothing," said David. "He wouldn't say what it was."

"And I wish I knew what it was," said Luke. "I really

long to know. Because I didn't do anything that I know of. I wanted to, like – well, you can imagine the way you'd want to do something really horrible and get your own back. I kept thinking of things. But what can you do when you're tied up and need both your hands to stop the snakes dripping poison on you?"

"Nothing," David said, feeling a little sick. He looked at Luke's pale freckled profile and hoped he would not want to say any more about his prison.

"Somebody did something, and they blamed it on me," Luke said bitterly. "They always blame it on me."

"Just like they blame me," David said. "I say, Luke," he said, because he had suddenly thought of Mr Wedding's advice again. "You don't need to be grateful to me for letting you out, you know. I did it quite by accident."

"So you did," said Luke cheerfully. "And you happened accidentally to stand up for me to Chew and then quite by mistake to Wedding. Come off it, David. If I'm not grateful now, I never will be. What shall we do for the rest of the evening?"

X THURSQAY

The next morning, as David expected, Mr Chew was digging at the back of the house and the raven was hopping among the geraniums at the front, looking for worms.

David went back to his room and thought. Then, for the first time in his life, he dressed by choice in his neat clothes, to establish his image with the raven. It made him later than usual for breakfast. All his relations were there. Uncle Bernard took his watch out and glanced meaningly from it to David, but to David's relief he did not say anything.

Mrs Thirsk, after her battle with Mr Chew, was looking decidedly stormy. She thumped down David's sausages and, as her habit was, glared at him to suggest that it was all his fault. David supposed she was right. If he had not let Luke out, none of the rest would have happened.

Uncle Bernard for once had a real disease. He told Astrid hoarsely that she had better not come near him or his sore throat would be the death of her – scoring one and one bonus-point, both unfair, because the time for the contest was supper, not breakfast. Astrid was taken by surprise and for a moment could not think of a disease at all.

"One of your heads," David suggested, in a purely sporting spirit.

Astrid glared at him. And David discovered a surprising thing. Mr Wedding's advice seemed to have been working slowly on him overnight. Now he knew he need not be grateful to her, Astrid could glare at him all she pleased and he did not mind. He simply ate his sausages and even knew that underneath Astrid did not care what he had said. She was really quite glad he had saved her having to answer Uncle Bernard's sore throat.

Mrs Thirsk meanwhile stood stormily by the door. "I've thought it over," she announced. "And my notice stays given unless that Chew leaves."

"Then I think, Ronald—" said Aunt Dot.

"Now come, Mother!" said Cousin Ronald. "I can't sack the best gardener I ever had."

"Either he goes or I go," said Mrs Thirsk.

"In that case—" Aunt Dot got up and went majestically to the french window. "Come here, my good man," she called. Mr Chew shuffled down the lawn and stood enquiringly at the window. "Now, Ronald," said Aunt Dot. "Tell him."

"I shall do nothing of the sort!" said Cousin Ronald.

"Then I go," said Mrs Thirsk.

"And good riddance!" said Cousin Ronald.

"Ronald!" exclaimed Aunt Dot.

"I am really too ill for all this shouting," complained Uncle Bernard. "Dot, I must ask you to send Mrs Thirsk away or I shall be prostrated."

"Quite right, Father," said Cousin Ronald. "She started it."

"I did not!" said Mrs Thirsk.

"And him too," said Uncle Bernard, pointing fretfully at Mr Chew. "Sack them both."

Cousin Ronald thumped the table. "Now you're being absurd!"

Mr Chew stood with his little eyes flickering from person to person. David could have sworn he was enjoying setting them all quarrelling.

"Ronald, do be quiet," Astrid said. "My head's coming on with this noise."

"Oh, everything brings your head on!" Cousin Ronald shouted, turning on Astrid. "Go away if you can't stand it."

"I'm going," said Astrid, and she got up and went out.

David bolted his last half sausage, for now, if any time, was his chance, while Mr Chew was occupied in grinning beadily at his quarrelling relations. "Can I go too?"

"Don't interrupt, David. Yes, if you wish," said Aunt Dot.

David shot from the dining-room and through the hall. Quietly, he opened the front door and stepped out. The raven stopped searching for worms and watched him from behind a geranium.

"Do you like worms?" David asked it.

"Yes, if there's nothing else going," it answered.

"What do you like to eat best?" said David.

The raven looked at him with unmistakable interest, evidently wondering what kind of food David was good for. "My favourite food," it said, "is a nice fresh carcass. But those are hard to come by these days."

"How about biscuits?" suggested David.

"I eat most things," the raven said hopefully.

"Here you are then," said David, and he held out a crumbly half biscuit left over from the packet Astrid had given him.

"Thank you," said the raven. With great dignity, it climbed from the flowers and marched across the drive to David. It took the biscuit with something of a peck and a snap, which made David take his hand away quickly. "Much obliged," it said indistinctly, and after that the biscuit was gone. The raven looked up hopefully, but David had only two biscuits left and his plan meant using them later. He went back into the house, and, very pleased

95

with himself, galloped up to his room to change. In the dining-room, Cousin Ronald and Aunt Dot were loudly abusing Uncle Bernard. He could hear them right upstairs.

When he was changed, David carefully put the matches in one pocket of his jeans and the last two biscuits in the other. If he strewed them down the drive, four half biscuits should surely keep the raven occupied until he had got clear away. He went downstairs and through the front door again. The raven was rather busy hauling a mighty worm from the left-hand bed.

David, with great cunning, asked it: "Do you like biscuits?"

The bird's eye came round to look at him. "You asked me that before," it said. "I do, but I prefer worms. I'll be with you in a minute."

Sadly, David watched it drag the worm clear and finish it off in two swallows. So much for his clever plan. The raven was obviously going to know him whatever he looked like. All the same, he waited until the bird came stepping gravely towards him over the drive. He could not cheat it of its biscuits, for it had treated him very fairly after all. He laid the biscuits in a small pile in front of it and went back into the house.

The quarrel was still going on in the dining-room. David could hear Mrs Thirsk saying she was not going to put up with such treatment any longer. And he heard Mr Chew's voice too. He went out of the side door and into the garden. Given a bit of luck, he might get over the wall without being seen from the dining-room.

But the raven was now in the middle of the lawn, dragging out an even bigger worm.

David said a bad word under his breath and hurried to the front door.

In the middle of the drive, the raven was just finishing

the last biscuit crumb and looked up at him hopefully as he came out. "Any more?" it said.

"No, sorry," said David. "I say, are there two of you?"

"Yes," said the bird. "There are always two of us."

"Thank you," said David, and went indoors again. By this time, he was full of deep, surly anger against Mr Wedding. No wonder he had set such a short time limit. He couldn't lose. Or could he? David stopped short at the foot of the stairs. Mr Wedding had said David had not mustered all his resources yet, and that was true.

Slowly, thoughtfully, David turned and went along the passage to the kitchen. He was forbidden to go there, but it was a resource all the same. It was a dismal, blank room with white machines humming away round the walls and full of the dismal smell of Mrs Thirsk's cooking.

David went to the clean white refrigerator and looked inside. He thought, as he looked, that it was a pity that Aunt Dot would never be brought to understand the difference between bad things you just did and bad things you simply had to do. Aunt Dot would call this bad, impartially. The nearest thing he could find to a nice fresh carcass was a joint of mutton, waiting to be turned into bad food. David took it out and, with a gasp, because it was cold and clammy, pushed it up the front of his shirt and fled with it to the drawing-room. There he buried it carefully behind the silk sofa cushions to wait. Then, feeling very grim and daring, he went upstairs and knocked on the door of Cousin Ronald's and Astrid's bedroom.

"Who is it?" Astrid said peevishly.

"David," said David, and held his breath. Astrid sounded in the kind of mood when she would tell him to go away. In which case he would have to manage with the joint of mutton alone.

"Oh, come in if you must," said Astrid. And when

David went in, she asked unpromisingly: "And to what do I owe the honour?" She was sitting at the dressing-table putting in her contact lenses. There were dresses strewn everywhere, as if she had been trying them on, but she did not look as if she had been enjoying herself. Her face was white and pinched and discontented.

"I want to ask you a favour," David said daringly.

"I thought as much," said Astrid. "You only look friendly when you want something. You're just like the rest of them."

"I don't think I am," said David. He felt very uncomfortable. It was quite true that the only times he had ever thought of being nice to Astrid were when he wanted something – as he did now. He told himself that Astrid had never been nice to him either, but that did not prevent him feeling so uncomfortable that he thought he would go away without asking.

"Oh, don't look so sheepish," said Astrid. "I'm in a bad temper, that's all. What do you want? The moon, or only half of it?"

David smiled. "A quarter of it'll do." Now he was not grateful to her, he was beginning to see that Astrid was not so bad really. Perhaps that was why he had thought of asking her to help. "It's about Luke," he said. "I was supposed to meet him at the recreation ground at ten, and it's gone ten now. I wondered if you could drive me there."

"I'm surprised Your Majesty doesn't take a taxi," said Astrid. "O.K., if it's Luke I'll do it. Anything's better than sitting about here. You'll have to wait, though, while I change to a handbag that goes with this dress. I'll be down in five minutes."

"That's very kind of you," David said gratefully.

"It is, isn't it?" said Astrid, and she got up and shook about seventy useless objects out of a blue handbag into the middle of one of the beds. David reckoned that five minutes might see them all collected again, but you never knew with Astrid.

He went slowly downstairs. There were sounds from the dining-room as if the quarrel might be ending. David hoped devoutly that they would not all be out and looking for the mutton before Astrid had collected her things. He sat on the stairs and waited three minutes. The quarrel still grumbled on. David got up and went to the drawing-room, where he unburied the mutton from the cushions and carried it over to the window. The raven was now sitting on the gatepost.

"Hey!" David said cautiously. "I've got something better than biscuits this time. Here." He threw the mutton towards the gate. It landed on the drive with a sticky thump.

"Meat?" said the raven.

"Yes," said David. He stayed to watch the raven glide down beside the joint and then hurried out into the hall again, just as Astrid came downstairs, carrying a white handbag and jingling her car-keys.

"Ready?" she said.

"You back out," said David. "I'll only be a second."

Astrid went out of the side door to the garage. When he heard the garage door go up, David darted out also, to carry out the third cunning stage of his plan. The second raven looked up as he came running up the lawn, and flew away from him into a rose bush.

"It's all right," David said to it. "I was only coming to tell you that the other raven has a joint of meat on the front drive."

This raven did not speak to David. It was in too much of a hurry. It went up out of the rose bush with a clap and a scramble. David watched it wheel between the chimneys and plunge out of sight over the roof with an angry squawk. He laughed. Those ravens were not going to think of following Astrid's Mini for some time. He ran back down the garden and got into the car.

Astrid backed past the house and the front garden. To David's delight, the ravens were quarrelling fiercely, tugging the mutton this way and that along the drive. Several passers-by were looking over the gate, for joints of mutton do not lie on people's drives every day.

"What huge birds!" said Astrid. "What have they got?"

"It looks like a lump of meat," said David.

"I wonder where it came from," said Astrid, but she did not stop to investigate. She put the Mini into forward gear and drove up the road.

"It is kind of you to drive me," David said thankfully.

"Don't mench," said Astrid. "What else have I to do? You should ask me oftener, David. To tell you the truth, I feel so sick of everything that I'd go anywhere, do anything, like the adverts say. I suppose it was my own fault for getting so set on going to Scarborough."

"That was kind of you too – not to go," David said awkwardly.

"Not my decision," Astrid said, turning into the main road. "Your Uncle Bernard didn't want to go, and what he wants he gets. Mind you, I never saw why you shouldn't have come too, but no one ever listens to a word I say, so that was that. Honestly, David, sometimes when they all start I don't know whether to scream or just walk out into the sunset."

It had never occurred to David before that Astrid found his relations as unbearable as he did. He asked with great interest, rather experimentally: "Why don't you do both? Walk into the sunset screaming?"

"Why?" said Astrid. "Because I'm a coward, David. I've no money, or I'd have gone years ago."

"I'd go," said David, "if I was old enough, whether I had any money or not."

"I've guessed that all right," said Astrid. "Bottom of the pecking-order, that's you. I'm next one up. We ought to get together and stop it, really, but I bet you think I'm as bad as the rest. You see, I get so mad I have to get at someone."

"I get at Mrs Thirsk," said David.

"More fool you. And she makes things pretty unpleasant for you, doesn't she?" said Astrid. "Oh, wasn't it marvellous when the Abominable Chew hit her with the spade? I nearly raised a cheer!"

"And me," said David. By this time, he was feeling so friendly towards Astrid that he said: "You know, you ought not to play so fair in the illness-contest. Uncle Bernard's always getting bonus-points for pretending to be sorry for you."

Astrid burst out laughing. "Well I never! The things you notice!" She laughed so much that she did not see the Wednesday Hill traffic lights turn green and David had to tell her. "So what do you advise me to say?" she said when they were moving again. "Mind you, I do get awful headaches," she added, in case David should think it was only a game.

"Yes, but you should say they're infectious and Uncle Bernard shouldn't come near you," said David. "And that sort of thing."

"All right," said Astrid. "You watch me this evening. And tell me what you make the score afterwards."

They were very pleased with one another when Astrid turned the Mini into the gates of the recreation ground and bumped across to the parking space. "There," she said, putting on the handbrake. "Where's Luke?"

The nearest thing was a boys' game of cricket, with Alan batting. Beyond that, there were people just mucking about, or playing football in spite of the heat, and beyond that again was official cricket, in whites. Luke, of course, was not there.

"I'll wait," said Astrid. "If he doesn't turn up, I can drive you back." She opened her handbag and took out her cigarettes. David grinned. "Bother!" she said, scrabbling about among the seventy useless objects. "Where are my matches?"

"I've got one," said David, nearly laughing. "Here." He struck one of his matches and held it towards Astrid's cigarette.

"Thanks," she said, puffing out a cloud of smoke. "Oh, here's Luke."

Luke was sauntering towards the Mini, smiling. David put his matches in his pocket and flung open the car door. He had one foot on the grass, when Luke stopped smiling and began to back away. Before David was properly through the door, Luke turned and ran, and a tall man with red-fair hair came from behind the Mini and ran after Luke in great strides.

David got out of the car and watched helplessly. Luke scampered for his life, but the tall man overhauled him steadily and easily, stride by stride. Luke might have had a start of twenty-five yards. Before he had scurried ten yards, the tall man had halved the distance between them. In another five, he had halved it again. Well before they came to Alan's game of cricket, he reached out and caught Luke's arm, and swung Luke nearly off his feet. Luke stumbled round to face him, rather defiantly, and the tall man laughed. To David's surprise, so did Luke.

"Who's that?" Astrid asked.

"I don't know," David said. His first thought, that the man was another of Mr Wedding's resources, dwindled to mere bewilderment when Luke laughed. Now the tall man was talking to Luke in a way that showed he liked him, and Luke was answering as if he were pleased to see him. Yet David saw Luke make two attempts to get away. The tall man stopped him each time by grabbing his arm again, and each time it happened he laughed. And Luke laughed too, as if it were a game. Another puzzling thing was that David was fairly sure this man had been one of the people looking over the gate at the ravens. That ginger-blond hair was hard to mistake. If so, David thought he must be a very fast runner indeed to cover three miles almost as quickly as Astrid's Mini.

"Go and find out," Astrid suggested.

David set out towards the two at an uncertain trot. They seemed to be arguing now. Luke was protesting about something and seemed very much less amused.

As David came within earshot, he heard Luke say: "I tell you I've no idea where it is. I never even knew you'd lost it." Seeing David coming, he said: "David, I told you last night that I didn't do anything, didn't I?"

"Yes, you did," David said.

The tall man let go of Luke's arm and turned to David. "Hallo," he said. David saw why Luke had seemed so pleased to see him. He had seldom seen a more generous, friendly face, or a nicer smile. "It was a good idea, that meat," the man said, laughing. "You thought you'd got clean away, didn't you? I'm sorry to disappoint you, but I had to talk to Luke."

"What are you going to do with him?" David said.

"Nothing," said the man. "He's all yours for today. You've earned it." Then he turned to Luke. "Off you go then," he said. "I'll take your word for it and think again, but I doubt if the rest of them will. Watch out after today, won't you?"

"Thanks," said Luke. "I will."

He and David strolled back to the car, and David was more puzzled than ever.

"What was all that about?" Astrid wanted to know. "Who was he?"

"One of my relations," said Luke. "He's lost something and he thought I knew where it was." To David, he added: "And I see why Wedding's so set on finding me now. It's rather a mess."

"He looked nice, your relative," said Astrid. "Is he Swedish or something?"

"Not specially Swedish," said Luke.

"That hair of his made me think he was," said Astrid. "I envy him that red-gold. It's a much nicer colour than mine."

"Impossible!" Luke said promptly.

"You!" said Astrid. "What are you two going to do? Do you want me to drive you somewhere?"

"Yes, please," said David. "Somewhere near the river," he suggested, thinking of the green river at Wallsey.

"Hop in then," Astrid said cheerfully.

David began to wonder how he had managed to misjudge Astrid so for all these years. He supposed it must be because she had to live with his relations too, and he had been lumping her in with the rest without thinking. She drove them to the river, where it was wide and brown and overhung with willows. When they began to be hungry, which happened rather soon with Luke, she telephoned Aunt Dot to say she was taking David and Luke out to lunch. They lunched off fish and chips out of paper bags in a way which would have horrified Aunt Dot had she known, and then returned to the river for the long, hot afternoon. Astrid sprawled on the bank in the sun, while David and Luke waded over to a reedy island and hunted for mussels.

They had a stack of blue mussels – which were getting a little smelly – when David happened to glance across at

Astrid. The tall man with ginger hair was sitting on the bank beside her, talking and laughing.

David nudged Luke. "Look. Is he really all right?"

"Oh, *he's* all right." Luke stood under a cloud of flies up to his knees in water, looking across the river. He spoke cheerfully, but he was thoughtful somehow. After a while he said: "He probably came to make sure no one else did. He said today was safe, and when *he* says a thing he means it. But I don't like it. Wedding would never have agreed if he wasn't pretty sure he could find me when he wanted."

David rubbed his face with a mussel-scented hand and knew for certain that he would not be able to elude Mr Chew and two ravens twice in a row. "Luke," he said, "don't you think you'd better go while he's here and you're safe? And I won't strike a match till Monday. Wouldn't that be best?"

"Oh drat!" said Luke, looking quite as mournful as David felt. "I think you're right. Just as we were enjoying ourselves too. The trouble is, I've remembered what it must be that I did. It's the only thing I can think of, so it must be. And the person I did it for is dead – years ago – and I shall never be able to prove it wasn't me. I shall just *have* to keep out of the way."

"Creep off now," said David, "and I'll see you Monday. Mr Wedding promised me he wouldn't put you in prison or punish you if he couldn't find you by Sunday."

"That does seem pretty watertight," said Luke. "Though, knowing him, there must be a catch in it somewhere. All right. See you Monday." He gave David his most engaging smile and waded quietly up among the tall reeds until he was hidden by them. For a second or so, David could hear his footsteps swishing in reeds and water. Then there was no noise except the river and Astrid laughing over the water.

David sighed. For twenty minutes or so he stayed sadly pottering about on the reedbank, to give Luke time to get away. Friday, Saturday and Sunday already seemed like three years. He left the mussels to rot and went back to Astrid.

The ginger-haired man looked up and smiled as David came wading alone across the river. "Luke gone?" he said. David nodded. "Can't say I blame him," the man said, and got up to go too. "I'll see you both again," he said, and shook David's river-scented hand before he went striding away along the river bank.

"David, you stink," said Astrid. "Like a fishmonger. You need a bath. Come on."

They drove home, and David had a bath because he felt he owed it to Astrid. But he felt sad. Monday was months away. He still felt sad when Cousin Ronald announced that he had sacked Mr Chew. He did not feel really alarmed when Aunt Dot said:

"David, I want to ask you about a joint of meat."

"You mean that meat that was in the drive?" said Astrid.

"I do," said Aunt Dot. "It came from our refrigerator."

"How queer!" said Astrid. "But David doesn't know any more about it than I do. We both saw it when I was driving him out to meet Luke, and we both wondered about it like anything, didn't we, David?" Then, before Aunt Dot could say more, Astrid turned to Uncle Bernard. "Poor Dad-in-law," she said. "I've never seen you look so frail. Do you think you should go to bed? I do hope I haven't given you this sore throat of mine."

When Astrid was winning twenty-two to seventeen, Cousin Ronald told her angrily that he would send for an ambulance if she said another word.

XI THE FRYS

It was raining a little the next day, but the ravens still kept watch, one at the front and one at the back of the house.

"Those great birds make me nervous," Astrid remarked as they were finishing breakfast. "What do they think they're doing?"

"I don't suppose they think at all," said Cousin Ronald. He was in a bad temper because he had been forced to dismiss Mr Chew. "Their heads must be almost as empty as yours."

Astrid said nothing. She simply got up and went out of the room.

"Stupid woman!" Cousin Ronald called after her.

"She is tiresome," Aunt Dot agreed. "You have a great deal to put up with, Ronald."

"So has Astrid," David pointed out.

"Well!" said Aunt Dot.

"Go up to your room," said Uncle Bernard.

"I only said—" began David.

"Do as you're told, you rude little beast!" said Cousin Ronald. Red with anger he pounced on David, seized hold of his ear and forced him to stand up. When David stood up, they were rather ridiculous, since David was actually a trifle taller than Cousin Ronald, and this made Cousin Ronald angrier than ever. David was afraid he was going to pull his ear off.

Mrs Thirsk came in, looked at David with grim

satisfaction, and said: "Mr and Mrs Fry have called. Shall I show them to the drawing-room?"

"Yes of course," said Aunt Dot.

"I really can't meet these people," quavered Uncle Bernard, going frail on the spot.

But before Mrs Thirsk could move from the doorway, Mr and Mrs Fry came pushing jovially past her into the dining-room. David stared. They were two huge, glad people, larger than life, with bright fair hair and genial beaming faces. They seemed to fill the room. They laughed. Their voices rang out. Cousin Ronald let go of David's ear in a hurry, and Aunt Dot went to meet the visitors in the gracious manner she kept for meeting visitors.

Mr Fry put his arm round Aunt Dot. "We must get to know one another better, my dear," he said, regardless of Aunt Dot's rigid frigid face, and he laughed loudly. No one could have been more unlike old, courteous Mr Fry with the rose spray.

"And we've never met!" Mrs Fry said to Uncle Bernard, and she pushed him playfully in the chest. Uncle Bernard first yipped indignantly and then sank back in his chair, frail almost to vanishing-point. Mrs Fry turned and beamed on Cousin Ronald. She was even more over-powering than Mr Fry because she was very lovely as well as very large. She was like a huge poster of a film star. "I wish I'd met you before!" she said, and seized both Cousin Ronald's hands, which made Cousin Ronald go very pink and simper a little.

Mr Fry advanced glistening on Mrs Thirsk. "My friend!" he said. In spite of her protests, he forced Mrs Thirsk to the nearest chair and made her sit down. "No, no," he said. "Let's have no distinctions here. Sit, friend."

"No I never," said Mrs Thirsk. "Not in all my born. Never." And she sat there gasping.

Mrs Fry came on to David. David backed away. She

gave him a most peculiar feeling. It was not unpleasant, but it felt too strong for him. "Hallo youngster," she said gladly. "I like you."

"Er – thanks," said David, and he wondered who on earth these huge imposters could be.

Somehow, the Frys had them all sitting down, all looking half pleased, half unsure, even Aunt Dot. Mrs Fry talked cheerfully about the weather and about gardening. And David's relations, in a stunned way, talked too.

"Oh, by the way," said Mr Fry, laughing, "has any of you seen Luke? We seem to have lost him."

David's stomach tipped a little. He was now sure that the Frys were another of Mr Wedding's resources.

"I am also anxious to see Luke again," said Aunt Dot. "I have asked repeatedly—"

Astrid came into the room just then. She had put on a new dress, perhaps in honour of the visitors, but more probably, David suspected, because she was miserable. Her face had its most pinched, discontented look.

Both Frys took one look at her and burst out laughing.

Astrid, not unnaturally, went extremely red. "What's so funny?" she said.

Mr Fry was still laughing. But David distinctly heard Mrs Fry say to him, under cover of his laughter: "What shall we do with this one?"

David felt really angry. He wanted to bang their flaxen heads together. When both Frys got up to make Astrid sit down with the others, David jumped up too and took hold of Mr Fry by his large warm arm. "What did you have to laugh at Astrid for?" he said. "It's rude." Mr Fry looked down at him in surprise, with his blond eyebrows raised. "And don't you dare do anything to her, either," said David.

"My dear boy!" said Mr Fry, bubbling over with amusement. "I only laughed because she was miserable when there wasn't any need. And all I'd do to her would be to make her happier."

David thought he was odious, and he would have told him so, except that the french windows bumped open behind him at that moment and he turned to see why. Mr Chew quietly trudged in from the garden, with his hat misted in raindrops.

Cousin Ronald bounced up. "I told you to leave yesterday!" he said indignantly.

"Yes, but I came back, didn't I?" Mr Chew pointed out.

"Then I go," said Mrs Thirsk, bouncing up in her turn.

"No, no, sit down," said Mr Fry, and pushed her back into her chair.

"Mr Fry!" Aunt Dot said majestically. "I—"

But the door to the hall opened and Mr Wedding came in. One of the ravens was sitting on his shoulder. Aunt Dot stared. "Good morning," Mr Wedding said pleasantly. "There's actually no need to keep everybody here, Fry. I've found some of the answers."

"Which of them did let Luke out?" said Mrs Fry.

Mr Wedding's one strange blue eye met David's. "That was David," he said. "He admitted it quite readily. It appears it was an accident."

"Accident!" said Mr Chew. "Well, I got the right one anyway."

David realised that when Mr Wedding took him out to lunch, he had not even been sure that David was the person he wanted. He had made David admit it by being friendly, just as Luke had feared. "You cheated me," he said. "You pretended you knew anyway."

"Don't get angry," Mrs Fry said soothingly. "That's his way. He's done that to cleverer people than you in his time."

"All the same—" said David, not at all soothed.

"Quiet, boy!" said Uncle Bernard. "Mr Wedding, will you please be good enough to explain this intrusion."

"Certainly," said Mr Wedding. "It shouldn't take long. All I want is for David to show me how to find his friend Luke."

"Then in that case," said Uncle Bernard, "as I am an old man and ailing, you know, I think I shall go upstairs." Looking his very frailest, he got up vigorously and tottered swiftly out of the room. David felt rather glad he had gone. He would only have made things even more difficult if he had stayed.

"And may I go?" enquired Mrs Thirsk. "I'm not staying in the room with that Chew, so I warn you."

"Get out then," said Mr Chew. "Or I'll give you some help."

Mrs Thirsk gave him a nasty look and swept out to the kitchen.

"It gives me great distress," stated Aunt Dot, "that David should be causing this trouble. I hope he has done nothing very wrong, Mr Wedding."

"Nothing at all," said Mr Wedding. "Luke's the one who's done wrong."

"Then you're abetting a criminal, David," said Cousin Ronald. "You'll be lucky to stay out of Court and I wash my hands of you. The one thing I won't tolerate is criminal practices. Come on, Mother. Get up, Astrid. Let's leave the brat to it."

"I advise you to make a clean breast of it, David," Aunt Dot said as she got up.

"Are you two really going?" said Astrid. "You know David's in a mess and all you can think of is to leave him to it!"

"Naturally, if David had committed the crime, I should stand by him," said Aunt Dot, progressing to the door. "But we have Mr Wedding's assurance that the criminal is Luke. I must say I am disappointed in Luke. I thought he was a nice child." She had reached the door by this time. Mr Fry, looking highly amused, held it open for her, and Aunt Dot nodded frigidly to him as she marched out. Cousin Ronald dodged out after her under Mr Fry's arm. Mr Fry shut the door behind them with a flourish.

David was neither surprised nor sorry that they had gone, but he was a little uncomfortable when Astrid stayed where she was. She, like the others, was assuming this was a police investigation, and David knew it could be nothing of the kind.

"Don't you try to put any twist on David," she told Mr Wedding, "or you'll have me to reckon with. He's only a kid."

"Bravo!" said Mr Fry.

"Shut up, you!" said Astrid. Mr Fry laughed so heartily that he made Astrid feel awkward. She opened her handbag and pretended to look for something.

"Now David," said Mr Wedding, "I suggest we fetch Luke."

"No," said David. "I'm not going to and you can't make me."

"Don't be so sure of that," Mr Chew said nastily.

"No you don't!" Astrid said. She had an unlit cigarette in her mouth and she glared at Mr Chew across it. "You try it, mate! David, have you got a match? I've lost mine again."

"No," said David. "Find your own. You've not looked." Astrid bent and sorted fruitlessly through her bag. Panic began to rise in David as he realised just what a danger to Luke that unlit cigarette was. He looked in a hunted way from the pity beaming in the faces of the two Frys, to Mr Chew's beady stare, and on to Mr Wedding. The raven was looking at him in an interested manner, but Mr Wedding was watching Astrid.

"Would you like to go and find some matches?" Mr Wedding said to her politely.

"No, it's all right," said Astrid. "You don't get rid of me like that. David's got some matches. I won't tell, David."

"Uncle Bernard will smell it if you smoke in here," David said desperately.

"Who cares about that old so-and-so?" said Astrid. "Come on, David. I'm dying for a fag."

"Smoking," said David, "is very bad for you."

"I know," said Astrid. "I know. David, I heard your matches rattle just now. Hand them over."

"Doctors have proved it's bad for you," David said, wishing she would take a hint.

"David," said Astrid, "just throw me those matches of yours and I'll throw them straight back. Promise."

There seemed no help for it. David did not dare protest any more in case the others realised why he did not want to strike a match. Perhaps it would do no harm if Astrid struck it for herself. Reluctantly he took out the box. Most reluctantly he tossed it over. "Here. Catch."

Mr Wedding caught it, smiling. "Allow me," he said. Courteously he opened the box, took out a match and struck it.

"Thanks," said Astrid.

The next second, Luke was standing in the window looking alarmed and uncertain.

"Run, Luke!" shouted David. "Quick! It wasn't me!"

Luke turned to bolt without a word. Mr Chew dashed across the room to stop him, but before he got near the window Luke was dragged back through it, struggling between the lady chauffeur and another lady who looked rather like her.

"Bring him here," said Mr Wedding. Politely he passed

David his matches back. "Thank you, David." David hardly had the heart to take them. Luke's face was so white you could see every freckle singly. David had a feeling his own face was rather pale too. He kept thinking of those snakes.

"Oh, David, I'm sorry!" said Astrid. "And here was I trying to help you."

David did not really attend to her. He was trying to follow Luke, who was being dragged further away across the room, and Mr Chew and the Frys were milling about in front of him, making it difficult. Astrid, puffing on her disastrous cigarette, followed David, still apologising and asking him what was going to happen to Luke. David wished he knew. There seemed to be a great many more people round Luke now and they were all very angry.

"Tell us what you did with it," said Mr Chew.

"He's bound to start lying," said Mrs Fry. "Make him tell the truth for once in his life."

"The truth, Luke," said Mr Fry.

"I didn't do it," said Luke. "It wasn't me."

"You always say that," said Mrs Fry.

Most of the other people were shouting accusations at Luke at the same time. David did not notice much about them except that they were tall and angry and that one man had only one ear. Nor did he notice particularly where they were, though he had a feeling that they were no longer in Uncle Bernard's dining-room but somewhere high up and out of doors. The chief thing he noticed was how small and frightened Luke's harrassed figure looked among them. Never had David felt for anyone more. It was just like himself among his own relations.

The similarity struck Astrid too. "He looks just like you when we all go on at you," she said. "It's making me feel awful!"

In fact, it was more official than a mere family row. The tall people, angry though they were, were standing in a ring to which David was sure there was some kind of order. Luke, in the middle and firmly held by the two ladies, was more like the prisoner at the bar than anything else. David was sure of it when a girl with red hair like Luke's came from what seemed to be the lower end of the circle, looking rather frightened, as if she was breaking the rules, and tapped Luke on the arm with an encouraging smile. Luke smiled back, in spite of his unhappiness, and David almost envied him.

"That will do," said Mr Wedding. The girl, looking even more frightened, went back to her place and left Luke on his own again. Mr Wedding stood at the head of the circle with the Frys and Mr Chew. He was taller even than the Frys, and darker, and more complicated, and David could see he had more powers, in a more mysterious way, than anyone else there. "Luke," he said, and Luke looked up at him hopelessly, "I want a confession from you."

"I didn't take any revenge," said Luke. "I swear it."

"Be careful what you swear to then," said Mr Wedding. "If you didn't hide it, why could a mere child set you free? Answer me, and tell me where it is."

"I can't," said Luke. "I don't know."

"Oh, put him back in prison!" said Mrs Fry, and the rest of the circle took her up. "Shut him up again. Make sure he suffers."

Mr Wedding waited until they had stopped. Then he said, in a sad, grim way, like a judge pronouncing the sentence: "You've brought us down to your own level, Luke, by doing this, and because of that, unless you can put it right, you'll have to go down to a deeper prison and a worse punishment than before."

This was too much for Luke. "Oh, *please* not prison again!" he said. "If you don't care how horrible it was, don't you think at least I've been there long enough to pay for *any* crime?"

"Not for what *you* did," said Mrs Fry.

"But it was a mistake, an accident!" Luke said frantically. "I meant it as a joke – I didn't think for a moment it would kill him."

"Yes," said Mr Fry. "A very fine joke, to put the blame on someone else."

"I know. That was part of it," said Luke. "I wanted to do something impossible and make it no one's fault. But I *did* take the blame. I did give myself up and go to prison. What more do you want?"

"Either give back what you took or go to prison again," said Mr Wedding. "And you can stop denying you did it too."

Luke opened his mouth as if he wanted to deny it, but he seemed to realise no one would believe him if he did. He looked desperately round the circle, though whether he was looking for someone who sympathised or a chance of escaping, David could not tell. He did not find either.

David was so sorry for him that he shoved his way into the middle of the circle. "Look here," he said. "Luke told me he didn't do anything and I know he meant it."

There was a great silence, and everyone looked at David. Most of them were haughty and indignant. Luke gave him a harrassed smile. Mr Wedding also smiled, a curious secret smile, but not, it seemed, because he was glad to see David.

"I see I should not have let you keep those shells and stones," he said. "Take my advice and go away. Don't you realise by now that Luke has no conscience and has simply charmed you?"

"I haven't!" Luke said indignantly.

David knew that this was simply Mr Wedding not playing fair again and, though he suspected there was some trick behind it, he did not let it bother him. "That's got nothing to do with it," he told Mr Wedding. "If you want the truth, Luke told me he did do something. But it wasn't a revenge. It was for someone who's dead now and he can't prove it."

"How very convenient!" said Mrs Fry, who seemed to have her knife into Luke properly, in much the same way Mrs Thirsk had for David.

"But it's true," said Luke. "Someone came to me in prison and asked for a way to hide something so that it might never be found, and I told them. But they didn't say what they were hiding. It was a good thousand years ago, maybe more."

There was some murmuring at this, and the man with the ginger-gold hair said: "Yes, that fits. That could be it." David was a little surprised to see him, because he had not noticed he was there before.

"My dear Luke," said Mr Fry, "don't try to pretend you didn't know what you were hiding. You took such good care none of us should ask you about it."

"That was part of the charm," said Luke. "None of you could ask me in prison, and I couldn't tell you a thing until someone else told you first. I didn't want you finding it. Besides," he added, quite in his usual manner, "I'd got sick of you all coming and asking me things. You never left me alone."

"Then who was it asked you to hide it?" demanded Mr Chew.

"It'll never be found if I tell you that," said Luke. "That's part of the charm too."

"It would be!" said Mrs Fry. "Liar!"

"Now, now," said the ginger-haired man. "That gets

us nowhere." He turned to Mr Wedding. "I'm the chief sufferer after all. If I vouch for him, can Luke go free and try to undo the charm?"

Mr Wedding smiled at him and then looked at Luke in a way David thought was rather regretful. "I notice he hasn't offered to undo it," he said.

"*Can* you undo it?" Mr Chew asked Luke bluntly.

"No," said Luke wretchedly.

There was another great silence. The ginger-haired man looked nearly as dejected as Luke. Then Mr Wedding sighed and signalled to the two ladies to take Luke away. David had a feeling that Mr Wedding wanted to send Luke to prison about as little as Luke wanted to go.

"Can't anyone undo this charm?" David said.

"I doubt it," Luke said sadly over his shoulder as the ladies moved off with him. "Only someone who doesn't know what he's looking for."

"Then that's simple," said David. "I can find it for you."

The ladies stopped and looked enquiringly at Mr Wedding. Mr Wedding did nothing but stroke the raven on his shoulder and look grave. The ladies looked at one another and evidently wondered whether to drag Luke away or not.

"You'd never find it, David," Luke said. "I'd better come clean before you make any promises. I bargained to have it made as difficult as possible, you see, because I thought it might be a chance to be let out of prison, if I was the only one who could find it. But that all came to nothing, and anyway I guessed what it was yesterday, so I can't find it now. No one looking for it was to name any names and the thing itself was a secret. And I was to hide it somewhere where there was no time and not to know where that was. So you see?"

David did see, and he was daunted.

Mr Wedding stirred. "The truth at last," he said. "Have you told him all the conditions?"

"Yes," said Luke. "Truly."

"Then," said Mr Wedding, with just a trace of triumph in his manner, "what do you say, David, to another bargain on the lines of our first one? You find what was hidden before midnight on Sunday – you can have any help you need – and Luke goes free and unharmed until then and for ever after if you find it. What do you say?"

David hesitated. He had a feeling Mr Wedding had tried to lead up to this bargain all through, which meant there must be a catch in it. Probably it was simply impossible. But Luke was looking at him with such radiant eagerness that David had not the heart to refuse.

"Why give him such a short time?" asked the ginger-haired man, while David hesitated. "As this seems to be our one chance of finding the thing, and as so much of our powers are bound up in it, couldn't you give him a month?"

Mr Wedding, with his eye on Luke's expectant face, shook his head slowly. "No," he said. "You can have until Sunday, Luke. My arrangements are made. David, I think if you haven't found it by then, you never will do. Do you agree to the bargain?"

Luke was looking so wretchedly nervous by then that David said: "All right. I'll try and find it."

All the people in the circle shouted, and nearly all of them, even Mr Chew, advanced on David to thank him. But Mr Wedding took hold of David's shoulder and steered him very firmly away downhill towards the french window. Luke, drooping and white, came along with them beside Astrid.

"You'll have to forgive a trick or so," Mr Wedding said as they went. "I think this is a better bargain than the last, David. Keep those shells and stones in your pocket, by the way. They come from a place of power. You'll find they can take you back there, if you need to go, and anyone else you choose with you. And I'll do all I can for you. I want Luke free too." David looked up at him uncertainly and saw Mr Wedding was quite in earnest.

XII THE SISTERS

Aunt Dot and Cousin Ronald had gone out, which David thought was a stroke of good fortune. Luke seemed utterly exhausted and not in a fit state to meet anyone. Astrid told David to get out deckchairs for them while she wrung some lemonade and biscuits out of Mrs Thirsk. The three of them sat on the lawn, which was shining and wet in the sun. A rainbow was arched across the remaining clouds, staining a distant clump of trees.

Astrid astonished David by not demanding any explanation. All she said was: "It's too bad of them to expect a kid like you to find you don't know what in two days and a half!" David thought that put his impossible bargain in a nutshell. "If it wasn't for Luke," said Astrid, "I'd have stopped you offering. The worst of it is, I think I know what you're looking—"

Luke raised his white face. "Well, don't tell him," he said. "Please."

"Not I," said Astrid. "I shall keep biting my tongue. But when I think—"

"Talk about something else," said Luke. "You're going to let it out. I can see it coming."

Astrid laughed. "How well you know me, Luke!" She changed the subject and began to talk about the lump of meat on the drive yesterday. Luke, after a wary look at her, slumped down in his deckchair again and seemed to David to be recovering. He felt nearly as jaded as Luke himself. He could not even think where to start looking, and he was supposed to have found it by Sunday night. "And the way those birds were dragging it about!" said Astrid.

David could not help thinking she could have chosen a more tactful subject. He was pulling himself together to explain that he had had to feed the mutton to the ravens, when something black beat the air beside his ear and he felt a sudden weight on his shoulder. Very startled, he ducked away sideways. The raven, perhaps to keep its balance, or maybe as an affectionate gesture, seized David's ear in its beak. It pinched nearly as hard as Cousin Ronald.

"What do you want?" David said, half laughing and half annoyed.

The raven let go of his ear in order to speak. "Have you any more meat?" it said.

David was struck by a sudden splendid idea. "Quick!" he said excitedly. "Has either of you anything it can eat?"

They looked a little stunned. Then Astrid picked up her handbag. "Yes. Wait a minute." She scrabbled through the seventy useless objects, and the seventy-first was a packet of cheese-biscuits. David tore it open and fed the biscuits one by one into the raven's ready beak.

"There," he said at last. "That's all. Now can you do me a favour?"

The bird was leaning out from David's shoulder in order to see his face. "Of course," it said and, no doubt as a gesture of gratitude, tried to take David's nose in its beak.

David clapped his hand over his nose in the nick of time. "Well, you said to ask you if I needed to know anything," he said, "and I do need to. Where do I start looking for this thing Luke hid?"

"Oh," said the bird. "That's a difficult one." Gravely it stepped from David's shoulder on to the back of his deckchair in order to think about it. "If I were you," it said finally, "I should ask the three Knowing Ones under the tree."

"How do I find them?" said David.

The raven thought again, making nibbling noises with its beak and raking at its sheeny head with its grey claws. "I can't explain," it said at last. David's heart sank. "The only thing I can think of," said the raven, "is for you to follow me and I'll lead you to it. Do you want to go now?"

"Yes please!" said David, and jumped up so quickly that he nearly knocked the raven off the chair. "Can we follow you in the car?"

"If you want to," said the raven, shaking its disordered tail feathers.

"Come on then!" David said excitedly to Luke and Astrid.

They got up, but slowly. "What has it told you?" said Luke.

"What on earth did it say?" said Astrid.

David was exasperated to find that neither of them could understand the raven. "Oh, it – get in the car and follow it and I'll tell you as we go," he said.

They hurried to the garage. Astrid's car-keys were the seventy-fourth thing in her bag. It came on to drizzle again while she was searching for them, but the raven obligingly waited on the garage roof until they were ready. Once the Mini was in the road, it flew steadily ahead towards the centre of Ashbury.

"Don't lose sight of it," said Astrid. "I can't watch it and drive too. Where are we going?"

"To find the three Knowing Ones under the tree," said David. "That's what it said."

"Of course!" said Luke. "I should have thought of that. But they won't tell you if they can help it. I wish I could come with you."

"A fine time to say you can't come!" said Astrid, going so fast round a corner that David and Luke were thrown against the windows. "Sorry. David, can't you make that bird understand that I have to slow down for corners?" The raven was keeping up its steady pace, flapping along the centre of the street, obviously quite unaware that cars could not do the same.

"I'll come as near as I dare," Luke protested, as soon as they were driving straight up the main road. "But they know me, and David won't get anywhere if I'm with him. They're three old women, David, and they're all blind, except for one eye that they share between them. Does that put any ideas into your head?" he asked, with a smile that showed he was nearly himself again. "You'll have to force them to tell you what you want to know, you see."

David smiled too. "Yes. I've read a story about that."

"It's not exactly a story," said Luke. "It happened. Twice. You'll be lucky to get away with it for a third time. But then I think you are lucky, if you can understand the ravens. Most people can't."

Astrid stamped on her brakes and said a word that would have turned Uncle Bernard very frail indeed. The traffic lights in front of them were red, but the raven, quite unaware of this, was flapping steadily off into the distance. "Get out and shout or we'll lose it," said Astrid.

David opened his door and scrambled out into the rain, but, before he could begin shouting, the raven came wheeling enquiringly back.

"Can't you jump over?" it called.

"No," David called upwards. "We'll have to wait." A number of people crossing the road looked at him as if he were mad.

Rather grudgingly, the raven waited for them in some

overhead wires. David could not get it to see the point of traffic lights. Each time they stopped, he was afraid they had lost it.

At the Wednesday Hill lights, Astrid became really puzzled. "Where does it think it's going?" she said. "If there's a tree on Wednesday Hill, I've yet to see it."

"Ah, but it won't *be* here exactly," said Luke. "I think it's going to the nearest way through."

"If you said that again in Greek, I might understand you," said Astrid.

The raven flapped steadily up crowded Wednesday Hill and then veered off into a side street which climbed to the very top of the hill. There were no trees there either. At the end of the street was a large shabby red-brick house with green railings in front. The raven perched on these railings. When Astrid drew up and David wound down his window, it said:

"It's in this house. You have to go downstairs, and it's the third door on the left. Can you find it now?"

"I think so," said David, very much dismayed. "Thanks."

"Good-bye then," said the bird and flew away over the roof of the house.

David told the others what it had said. "And I don't know what to do," he said. "I can't just walk into the house and ask them for their tree, can I?"

"Don't look so glum. We'll think of something," said Astrid cheerfully, collecting her bag and getting out. "Drat this rain on my hair! We'll say we've come about the drains. Luke'll think of something, won't you, Luke?" Luke nodded, quite as cheerfully, and seemed to have no doubt that he would.

But Luke had no need to think of anything. The door was opened by Alan.

"Oh, hallo," he said, recognising David and Luke.

"We weren't going to play cricket today because of this rain. Want to come in?"

David, delighted with this piece of luck, led the way indoors into a shabby hall paved with green linoleum. A row of four tubby little girls came out of a room and stared at them.

Alan said, in a resigned way: "Those are my sisters."

"How do you do?" Astrid said to them. They stared at her.

Then a woman who was plainly Alan's mother came out of the room behind the little girls, shunting the whole row of them forward like railway trucks. "Oh, good morning," she said to Astrid. "Have you come to look at the rooms?"

"That's right," said Astrid, with great presence of mind, long before David had gathered what Alan's mother could be talking about. "Would it be a nuisance if I were to look round them now?"

"Not at all," said Alan's mother. "They're upstairs. Would you like to come up and look?"

"I think my nephew would rather talk to your son," said Astrid.

"Of course," said Alan's mother. "Alan, you take him downstairs and show him your things. What about you?" she asked Luke.

"I'll look at the rooms," said Luke. With a wink at David, he followed Astrid and Alan's mother up the broad bare stairs. Alan's mother was saying things like: "I hope you don't mind the top of the house," and "We're in a bit of a mess just now."

David, feeling extremely foolish, went with Alan down some steep stairs at the back of the hall and fell over Alan's cricket bat at the bottom.

"Oh. Sorry," said Alan. He was feeling shy of David and did not know what to say.

"That's all right," said David, quite as awkwardly. It was a lucky fall. As he picked himself up, David noticed a door on the left at the bottom of the stairs which he would certainly have missed otherwise. That made one door. He followed Alan into a long basement room opposite and behind him, to his embarrassment, he heard the row of little girls trooping down the stairs after them.

"Don't mind them," said Alan. "What shall we do?"

The end wall of the basement was on David's left. In the middle of it was a fireplace and, on either side of the fireplace, was a cupboard built into the wall. That meant that the far cupboard was the third door on the left. Since there seemed nothing else to be done, David walked over to it. "Do you mind if I look in here?" he said, feeling an awful fool.

"It's only a cupboard," said Alan.

Feeling sillier than ever, David opened it. True enough, it was a cupboard, full of shelves. Half-heartedly David gave the nearest shelf a push. It moved backwards under his hand and, with it, the other shelves and the back wall of the cupboard. He pushed again. The whole wall, shelves and all, swung backwards like another door, letting in a shaft of clear, steady light, not quite like sunlight.

"I never knew it did that!" Alan said, looking over David's shoulder. "Shall we go through?"

"Yes," said David. "I've got to go anyway."

He stepped through the cupboard, and Alan followed him. Neither of them said anything when they were through. They looked round, looked up, and then looked at one another's awestruck faces.

It was the biggest tree imaginable, or more than that. Its giant roots rose above their heads, far above, like the rafters of a monstrous barn. Beyond them, they could see the huge twisted trunk of the tree, going up and up and up, higher than any mountain David could think of; and beyond that, so high that drifting clouds and distance made it hard to see, if they lifted their heads right back, they could just pick out the great shadowy spread of the leaves and branches – or perhaps guess at them more than see them. A tiny black speck was floating up there. David thought it could be the raven, but it was too far off for him to be sure.

After a moment to take it all in, he went forward under the roots and Alan kept close beside him. Still neither of them said a word. But it occurred to both of them at once to look round to see how they were going to get back to the basement. They saw a vast plain of grass, vanishing into blue distance. But, about twenty yards from them, the open door stood on its own in the middle of nothing, like a piece of stage scenery. They could see the grey light from the basement between the shelves. As they looked, first one of the little girls, then another, came wonderingly through the door, until they were all four standing in a row, staring.

Alan's face bunched up in annoyance. Then he shrugged. He and David turned and went cautiously round the nearest massive root.

Round the other side was like a rough and ready workshop. Near the root, almost in front of the boys, there was a well, very full of dark water, so that it almost brimmed over. They could see that it was very deep, because they could just pick out dim lines of stonework, going down and down and down. An old woman was rinsing wool at the well, wringing it out with strong, knotty hands. Alan stopped, with a gasp, and then relaxed as he realised she was blind. Her eyes were wrinkled slits. A second old woman sat on a root-stump behind her with a tall thing David thought might be a spindle. Wondering, they watched her set it going round, pulling, twiddling, waiting until there was sufficient tension, and then take wool from the head of it and feel it out into a growing thread. She was blind too. The third old woman was moving about behind them. She was taking threads of spun wool and hanging them over a root which stretched across the space like a gnarled beam. Every so often, one thread slipped off the beam, and she caught it, wound it neatly on a wooden bobbin, and stacked it in a recess under another root. Sometimes she pulled at a thread and, if it did not come down at once, she took a pair of scissors from her pocket and cut it. Then she wound it up. Some of the threads were bright colours, but most of them were the yellowish white of undyed wool.

The old woman at the well remarked: "There are strangers near."

"Well, it was today we were expecting them, wasn't it?" the spinning-woman answered in a matter of fact way. "Don't tell them anything."

"Of course not, dear," said the washing-woman.

"They're only children," the old woman at the beam said. "Six of them." As she had not turned round to look, David could not think how she knew. But he realised she must be the one with the eye. He felt rather helpless. If she knew so much without looking, he could not see himself ever taking her by surprise.

Alan's four sisters had come quietly up by now. They stood in a row, staring at the three old women.

"What are you doing?" said one of them at last.

"Leos for medlars to make little girls wonder," the spinning-woman answered.

"Run away, dears," said the washing one.

"Are you witches?" asked another sister, with interest.

"What do *you* think?" said the old woman at the beam, and she put her scissors in her pocket and her hands on her hips and limped forward until she was almost beside

David and Alan. "Run away, dears," she said, looking round at the six of them.

The little girls stared at her. "You've only got one eye," one of them said.

"You're luckier than me. You've got two," the old woman said.

"Why haven't the other ladies got eyes?" persisted the little girl.

"Oh bother!" said the spinning-woman. "I wasn't thinking what I was doing, with their chatter. I've a great tangle come in my yarn."

"Do you want the eye, dear?" asked the one who had it.

"Yes, please, dear," said the spinning-woman.

David could not help smiling. These four dim little girls had done what he could never have done by himself and convinced the Knowing Ones that the strange children were all harmless. He thought he would never again despise them, or anyone else, for being stupid.

The old woman took the eye out. It came out rather more easily than Astrid's contact-lenses and in much the same way. Alan, who had never seen Astrid take a lens out, looked sick. The little girls were astonished.

"I can't take my eyes out like that," said the eldest.

"What are you going to do with it now?" asked the youngest.

"Give it to my sister," said the old woman. "Where's your hand, dear?"

"Here," said the spinning-woman, holding out her strong bent hand.

David moved quicker – and ten times more quietly – than he had ever moved in the slips. He flung himself forward, picked the eye out of the old woman's fingers, and retreated beyond the well before the spinning-woman realised it had gone.

When she did, she raised a shriek which made David's ears quiver. "Where's the eye? Who's got it? Children, who's got the eye?"

"He took it," said one of the little girls, pointing at David. Of course the old women could not see her point. They wrung their hands and stumbled about, searching frantically.

"Keep it warm, whoever you are!" shrieked the spinning-woman.

"It's our only eye," whimpered the washing-woman. "Give it to my hand here." She held her hand out in Alan's direction. "I'll tell you anything you want to know if you put it in my hand again."

David was appalled at the distress he had caused them. He had half a mind to give the eye straight back. It felt so nasty – rather like a warm, firm oyster, and much bigger than he would have expected. He looked down at it. It looked back, blue and difficult and deep. David jumped. He could have sworn it was Mr Wedding's other eye and that it could see him. He put it behind his back.

"I've got it," he called out. "I'll give it back if—"

Without a pause to think where his voice came from, they all turned round and came straight towards him.

David backed away. "Careful. You'll fall in the well."

But they avoided the well easily and hurried towards him with their muscular arms stretched out to take hold of him. David dashed away sideways and round among the little girls. Alan suddenly backed him up by rushing noisily away in the other direction. The Knowing Ones stopped, confused.

"What are you doing?" a little girl asked David.

That brought the old women after him again.

"Stay where you are!" he shouted. "Or I'll wave the eye about till it's cold. Then I'll throw it down the well."

They stopped just beyond the well, holding one

another's bent hands for support, and he could see he had defeated them.

"What did you want to know?" asked the one who had had the eye.

"How to find the thing that Luke hid," said David. "But you mustn't tell me what it is or who hid it."

"Luke hid many things in his time," said the spinning-woman. "How do we know which you're asking about?"

"That's just putting me off," said David. "You know. The thing Mr Wedding wants to find. It belongs to the ginger-haired man who caught Luke on Thursday."

"That's a difficult question," said the washing-woman. "It's hidden out of time, you know."

"Luke told me that," said David. "But I have to find it."

"Very well," said the third old woman. "Go to Wallsey again. Cross the bridge and go into the hall on the island. You must ask the one with the dragon about him where to look. He knows who hid it. That's the truth. Now can I have the eye back, please?"

"Here you are," said David. "Thanks." A little nervously, he went up to the three old women and put the eye into the nearest of their three outstretched hands. The one who got it was the one with the scissors. As her crooked fingers closed on it, David retreated smartly in case of trouble.

But all the old woman did was to put the eye in – again rather as Astrid put in a lens – and to stare intently first at David, then at the four little girls, then at Alan, who was coming slowly back from the distant spaces under the root.

"There's a goat, or something, there, eating a root," he said.

The old woman turned to David again, and very piercing that eye was, worse than Mr Wedding's. "So it's you," she said. "You fooled us properly. Well, go in peace, but

132

don't think the rest of your life's going to be easy. You'll see a face tomorrow you won't forget in a hurry."

"Thanks" David said doubtfully. "Come on, Alan. Get your sisters. We've got to go." Quietly and thoughtfully, almost sadly for some reason, he turned and went back to the cupboard door in the middle of the grass, followed by Alan and his string of sisters. The cupboard door closed with a final kind of snap behind the last of them.

In the basement, David said good-bye to Alan and promised to meet him later. He found Astrid and Luke waiting for him when he came up the stairs, and they both seemed very jolly, particularly Astrid.

"I've got a surprise for you that Luke thinks you might like," she said when they were in the car. "Did you get what you want?"

David told them everything except what the old woman said at the end. He felt that was private.

Luke was delighted, but he also seemed very surprised about the man at Wallsey. "*He* knows!" he said. "I'd no idea – oh, now I begin to see!" He started to laugh.

"Can we go to Wallsey this afternoon?" David asked Astrid.

"No go," she said. "Tomorrow morning. I have to go out."

David was rather disappointed, but he felt he could not complain. Luke did not seem worried by the delay, and Astrid had been so kind already that he did not like to grumble.

"Now for it," said Astrid, as the Wednesday Hill lights turned green. "David, I've been thinking – ever since last Sunday really. You started me off when you suddenly rounded on me and asked me how *I'd* like to be packed off to Mr Scrum. And I saw your point. Then this morning, when they were all on to Luke, I saw it clearer than ever. I have a bad enough time of it, but you get it even worse, don't you? How would you like it if we both got out – you and me -- and lived somewhere else?"

When somebody throws a totally new idea at you, it is hard to know what to say. David's first idea was to swing round and look at Luke. It seemed to him that this might be Luke's way of paying him back for offering to undo the charm.

"Astrid thought of it," Luke said sweetly, and David knew perfectly well then that Luke had prompted Astrid.

"Those rooms I saw," said Astrid. "They're really nice – almost a top-floor flat and cheap as things go nowadays. So I took a chance and told her we'd take them. Keeping my fingers crossed and hoping you'd agree, because I can't see myself managing alone and I don't want to leave you to your fate with Bernard and Dot. What do you say?"

David did not say anything, although he did not notice he had not spoken. What a marvellous thing, to live in the same house as Alan! And what a pity he had sworn not to despise Alan's sisters!

His complete silence made Astrid nervous. "I shan't be offended if you say no," she said hastily. "You may think it's Hobson's choice after all, because you know what I'm like when one of my heads comes on, and I don't suppose we shall have any money and you'd have to leave that school. But I used to earn quite well as a typist, and I daresay I can do it again."

It dawned on David that he had not yet agreed. "I think it's a brilliant idea!" he said.

"Oh, I'm so glad!" said Astrid.

"You wait until he starts feeding ravens with the week's meat," said Luke.

XIII WALLSEY

Astrid drove home and Luke went into the house with them. As soon as Aunt Dot appeared, they both realised what a mistake this was, but Aunt Dot, to David's amazement did not seem to remember having been convinced that Luke was a criminal. She invited him to lunch. At lunch, Uncle Bernard complained of his liver, and Cousin Ronald that David had left three deckchairs to get soaked and ruin the lawn; and Mrs Thirsk that she had not been expecting a visitor. But none of them seemed to remember anything else.

David asked Luke about it, and Luke, with a rather secretive smile, remarked that both Mr Wedding and the Frys were good at making people forget things.

However it happened it was fortunate, because the real Mr and Mrs Fry called that afternoon. David was forced to sit in the drawing-room and be polite to old Mr Fry's courtesies. Mr Fry was interested in David. He talked to him the whole time, which was difficult, because Mr Fry's interest in cricket was plainly only polite. But it was over in the end. David and Luke wandered off together and both of them forgot that Luke was only free until Sunday night.

Next morning, Astrid announced that she was taking David out on a trip to Wallsey. It caused an immediate outcry from the other three.

"I can't think why you want to take David to a vulgar place like that," said Aunt Dot.

"On a Saturday, of all times!" said Cousin Ronald.

"Why take him anywhere?" said Uncle Bernard.

"If you remember," Astrid said, somewhat in the same loud, polite way David had told them they could leave him on his own, "*if* you recall, we decided not to go to Scarborough because David was at home. And if you think looking after David means telling him to mind his manners at meals, I don't. I think it means taking him about and taking an interest in him. So I'm going to Wallsey. With David."

"I can't possibly let you go to a low place like that on your own," Cousin Ronald said crossly. "You might be annoyed by trippers or – or people. If you insist on going, Astrid, I shall insist on coming too."

"She won't be alone. I'll be there," David pointed out.

"Don't talk nonsense," said Cousin Ronald. "It's Saturday, Astrid, and the place will be crowded out. You'll be jostled. You'll get one of your heads."

That was attacking Astrid on her weakest side, but, to David's gratitude and admiration, she stood firm in spite of anything the other three said. David thought this must be the first time he had ever been truly and spontaneously grateful to any of his family, and it gave him a rather odd feeling. Then, to his dismay, he found that Cousin Ronald was standing firm too.

"I'm not having you go and waste my good money on trash," he said, which David suspected was his real reason for standing firm. "Go if you insist, but I shall come too and make sure you don't squander the earth on hot-dogs."

And come he did. When Astrid backed the Mini out of the garage, Cousin Ronald got into the seat beside her and sat there looking firm and righteous. Astrid gave David a most meaning look as she got out.

"What are you getting out for?" Cousin Ronald demanded.

"To let David in," said Astrid. "There are only two doors." She gave David a wink and put a cigarette in her mouth. "Match, David?"

David laughed as he got out his box and struck a light for her. It was extraordinary how much nicer Astrid was than his other relations. Living alone with her promised to be great fun.

Cousin Ronald was in a very bad temper at being forced to come with them. "Put that thing out!" he snapped. "Filthy habit!"

But by this time, Luke was strolling across the road. David blew out the match and Astrid put the cigarette away. "Hallo," said Luke. "I see the clans are gathering." He was climbing into the Mini in front of Astrid, when Alan too appeared, riding a bicycle and looking uncertainly at the numbers of the houses.

"Hallo," he said to David. "How's your quest going?"

"We're just going to Wallsey," said David. "On the next bit."

"Can I come too?" said Alan.

David looked helplessly at Astrid. Luke leant out of the car and said: "Let him come. I think you'll need him."

"Are you sure you wouldn't like me to ask Mrs Thirsk along too?" Astrid asked tartly. "Car or bike, Alan?"

"Bike," said Alan. "Bet I beat you there." It was a good bike, with a good many gears. Alan wheeled round, ticking smoothly, and was away long before David had climbed into the car.

The way Astrid went to Wallsey was nothing like the way David went with Mr Wedding. She did not go through the centre of Ashbury but through the shabby outskirts beside the river. Shortly, they came to a wide gravelly space full of parked cars and hot-dog vans. Astrid backed the Mini into a space, and they were there. Alan was there also, leaning against the wall by the river. He waved to them.

David climbed out of the car in some bewilderment. He could see the lake over the wall Alan was leaning on. It was quite small, really only a place where the river widened, and, because it was a fine Saturday in the holidays, it was full of little coloured pedal boats and the pedal boats were full of screaming girls and shouting boys. There were warehouses on the other side of the lake and, on the near side, a white-tiled pub called The Rainbow. Beside the pub was an archway decorated with coloured lights and a neon sign above it which said *Wallsey Island Funfair*. The funfair was on the island in the middle of the lake. There David saw more coloured lights, the towering Big Wheel, roundabouts and stalls. Music and screaming came loudly across the water. For a moment, David seriously thought they had come to the wrong place.

"It's all right," said Luke. "It *is* here, I promise."

Cousin Ronald looked at the crowds of people in the car park, the boats and the noisy island, and sniffed the hot-dog scented air in the greatest disgust. "Well, what part of this palace of pleasure are you going to waste my money on first?" he said to Astrid.

Alan came up, saying: "Shall we hire boats? That's fun." Cousin Ronald shuddered.

"Go over to the island," David said. "I've got to find someone there."

"Crude, noisy and expensive," said Cousin Ronald. "I won't hear of it."

But David, Luke and Astrid were consulting about it, so none of them took any notice. "All go?" said Astrid.

"I can't," Luke said regretfully. "They blackballed me years ago. And I don't advise you to go either, Astrid. It's an all-male club, you see, and they might not let David in if you're with him."

"Well!" said Astrid. "What price Women's Lib!"

Luke chuckled. "Ask Wedding," he said. "It's nothing to do with me."

Astrid did not seem to mind too much. "We'll wait in the pub then," she said, "and let the other three go. Or do you want to go alone, David?"

David did not at all mind Alan coming, but he very much hoped that Cousin Ronald would decide to wait in the pub too. But this was not to be. Astrid said: "Ronald, we're going to sit outside the pub, while David asks about the—"

"Watch it!" Luke said sharply. Astrid clapped her hand over her mouth.

"Very sensible idea," said Cousin Ronald, noticeably relieved that Astrid was not threatening to spend money on dodgems and things. "Then I'll take the boys to the island, shall I? Give them a trip on the roundabout and then join you there."

"Thanks," David said glumly, and Alan added: "The Big Wheel's better."

"Roundabout or nothing," said Cousin Ronald jovially, leading the way towards the archway. "Just one ride, mind."

Alan looked at Cousin Ronald in a slow, considering way and David knew he was wondering how anyone came to be so stingy. He felt ashamed of Cousin Ronald, so much ashamed that he could not think of anything to say to Alan. They walked in a silent procession over a steel bridge looped with coloured lights with the little pedal boats splashing and screaming gaily beneath them.

Almost the first thing beyond the bridge was a roundabout. "Do you both want a ride?" asked Cousin Ronald, in a tone that meant surely they didn't.

Alan looked at David and understood that they were here for another reason. "No thanks," he said. David refused too, and winked at Alan. Alan might not be very clever – David was sure he was not – but he had the makings of a real ally. David began to like him very much. Alan winked back, and they wandered on, past rifle-ranges, hooplas and dodgem cars. Cousin Ronald was very jolly, now that he had not been asked to pay for the roundabout. He even offered them candy-floss. And when both of them refused, Alan with obvious regret, he became happier than ever and followed David without grumbling, while David walked down one alleyway and up the next in search of the hall.

It was a large, narrow building, open to the alleyway at one end. A notice over the opening said *Hall of Fun*. David went in without hesitating, and Alan went with him. Cousin Ronald followed, saying: "I can't think what people see in these places. It's sheer daylight robbery."

There were pinball machines along both walls and a fruit-machine at the entrance. The place was full of the musical thud, thud, thud of the balls hitting the pins, with the occasional long rattle when the fruit-machine gave up coins. There was music too, and much loud laughter from groups of young men with long hair who were working the pinball tables, shouting jokes and quite often rocking the machines ruthlessly to make sure they won.

"This is a very rough place," Cousin Ronald said. "Come along, boys. You can have a ride on the dodgems."

"Walk round that way," David said to Alan. "And if you spot someone with a dragon about him, come and show me."

They separated. Cousin Ronald followed Alan saying: "There should be a law against these machines. I refuse to let either of you spend a penny on them."

Left on his own, David walked casually round inspecting the various groups. A lot of the young men had jackets with emblems or pictures on the backs but, though David saw deaths heads, arrows, tigers and streaks of lightning, he saw no dragons at all. He looked at badges, flowing ties, bands round hair and patterns on shirts, without success. They were a very dressy lot, and very happy too. David was discouraged, although he was sure this was the right place. There were no girls or women in the groups – just noisy young men, enjoying life and cheating the pinball machines.

Alan was at the end of the hall watching a particularly noisy group cheating a machine called Wall of Death Spectacular. Two young men were having a contest and the others were cheering them on. David joined the group on the other side, and sighed with relief. One of the young men put out his hand to pull the lever and there was the dragon. He was wearing a short-sleeved sweater, so that it was quite obvious. The dragon was tattooed round and round his forearm, with its head on the back of his hand.

David let the young man have his turn – he was winning – and then reached out and took hold of him by his tattooed right wrist. "Excuse me," he said. "There's something I need to ask you."

The rest of the group were far too interested in the other young man's turn to notice, but the young man with the dragon turned and looked at David. David thought he seemed remarkably pleasant, fair and good-humoured and kind. "Now just who are you?" he said.

"My name's David Allard," said David. "The three Knowing Ones sent me to ask—"

"Wait a minute," said the young man. "You don't belong here do you?"

"No," admitted David. "But I know Mr Wedding."

"Don't we all?" said the young man, laughing. "But I can't tell strange kids like you anything unless the rest of them agree. That's the rule here. Was it urgent, what you wanted to know?"

"Yes," said David. "I've only got till tomorrow night."

"Well, I'll see what I can do for you," said the young man. He turned to the rest of the group. "Hey, you lot! There's a kid here wanting to ask me something. Says it's urgent."

Someone from the next pintable called out: "You know there's three of them, do you?"

"Then that's simple, isn't it?" said the one who was having his turn. He was not anxious to be interrupted. "Throw them all out."

"Come off it!" said the one with the dragon. "It's only two kids and an old fatso. And it's urgent."

They gathered in the central space, arguing about it in a good-humoured way. Before long, most of the other young men left their pintables and joined in. David stood back beside Alan to wait. Cousin Ronald came up to them.

"I think we'll leave now," he said. "We don't want these yobboes to beat us up, do we?"

"We can't. I have to ask him something," David said, pointing to the young man with the dragon.

"Who is he?" said Cousin Ronald suspiciously.

"I've no idea," said David. "But he's nice."

Here the group broke up, laughing and smacking the young man with the dragon on the back in a friendly way. He came back to David. "Sorry about this," he said. "You shouldn't be here at all, you see, any of you. But it's lucky there's three of you, because there's a rule that lets me talk if three people run the gauntlet first. Will you agree to that?"

"Yes," said David, though he had no idea what he was agreeing to.

"All right," said Alan loyally.

"Agree to *what*?" said Cousin Ronald.

"Run the gauntlet," said the young man. "It's a bit of a giggle really, but the boys won't hear of me talking to the kid unless you agree."

"A mature man like me," said Cousin Ronald, "does not play games. But since you make such a point of it, I'll agree for this once. As a great favour, mind. David, I hope you're grateful."

"Yes, I am," said David, though it was a feeling he had to struggle for rather, and quite unlike his gratitude to Astrid. He was fairly sure Cousin Ronald had only agreed because the young man with the dragon was so large and strong-looking.

As soon as they heard that the strangers had agreed, all the young men, with a lot of laughing and many jokes to the young man with the dragon about his past catching up with him, arranged themselves in two long lines up the centre of the hall and prepared to enjoy themselves thoroughly. They were two very long lines. David, as he began to see what they were in for, rather wished there had not been so many of them. It was surprising that the hall had room for so many – except that it was now no longer quite the same place. It was wider and loftier and longer. With what little attention he could spare from the jostling lines of young men, David saw carved pillars, painted recesses and the glitter of golden things on either side. But the end of the hall still opened into the fairground. People passed, eating candy-floss and toffee-apples, some hundreds of yards away there.

"Ready," called the nearest young man. "First one, please." And everyone in both lines began to clap in rhythm by way of encouragement. Clap clap clap-clap-clap.

"They do this to new-bugs sometimes," Alan said. "Want me to go first?"

Clap clap clap-clap-clap.

"No. I'll go," said David. He had seen it done too, but he had never been on the receiving end of it before.

Clap clap clap-clap-clap. David took a deep breath and

143

set off up the space in the middle of the two lines. He got a heavy, playful punch on the arm from each of the first pair. Then the same from the next pair. Next, an open-handed smack from one side and a tweak from the other. Clap clap clap-clap-clap went all the others. It was no good going too fast. The young men were all so strong that David knew he would be knocked off balance in no time if he started to run. Then his course would become a zig-zag and very much more painful. He kept down to a steady pace, and they did their good-humoured best to knock him sideways. They were very friendly about it. David did not mind too much until about the centre of the line, when a rather brutish-looking boy punched him unkindly in the stomach. David turned to say something, found the boy about to do it again, and went on hurriedly, with the clap clap clap-clap-clap ringing in his bruised ears. The young man with the dragon was right at the end of the line. David saw the dragon-coiled arm come out and winced away a little, because he looked the strongest of the lot. But the dragon-faced hand merely patted him on the head.

"You'll do," said the young man, laughing. Panting, David nodded and tried to laugh too. His upper arms ached, his ears fizzed and, judging by the hot, hard feeling, his top lip was very fat indeed. David licked it all the time he was watching Alan come up the line.

Alan took a faster pace than David. Being more solidly built, he could afford to. He also took the precaution of covering his head with his arms. That meant that he got a fair old drubbing in the ribs and over the shoulders, but all in all he probably had an easier time. When he got to the end, he grinned, felt his ribs carefully and then assured David he was all right.

"They could have hit a lot harder if they'd wanted to," he said.

Clap clap clap-clap-clap went the two lines. Down at the other end of the hall, Cousin Ronald refused to move. "Nothing will possess me to indulge in this brutish pastime!" he announced, rather shrilly.

The rhythm of the clapping changed. It became unmistakably the slow handclap.

"Uh-uh!" said the young man with the dragon. "Seen what he's in for, has he?" He shouted to the other end of the hall. "Get him moving then!"

The slow handclap grew louder. People called out. Then, as Cousin Ronald still refused to move, the two young men nearest him took him by the arms and slung him into the line. "Go on, you agreed!" one shouted.

Cousin Ronald bucketed into two hard fists and bounced off across the gap into two more. "I shall write to the papers!" he screamed. "Brutal louts!" The slow handclap grew louder and slower still.

David was so ashamed that he could hardly look at Cousin Ronald coming up the line. He did not mind too much what the young men thought – and it was clear what that was – because they were strangers. But Alan was not exactly a stranger, and Alan was trying not to laugh at Cousin Ronald's disgraceful progress. Cousin Ronald bumped and bounced up the line to that slow derisive clapping. He tried to dodge. He yelled. He cursed them. He tried to break out through the line and was hauled back. He groaned. He squeaked. He pleaded. Then, about the middle, he tried to put a stop to it by falling down and pretending to faint.

There was a great roar of derision. Everyone knew he was faking. Alan laughed in earnest, and the boy who had hit David in the stomach helped Cousin Ronald up with a boot in the rear which must have been quite painful.

They pushed him on again. And this part made David even more ashamed, for the second half of the line hardly hit Cousin Ronald at all. They made great swipes at him and ended up scornfully flipping him. They laughed, made catcalls and shoved and jostled him onwards. When Cousin Ronald staggered whimpering to the end, the dragon young man simply put a hand between his shoulders and shoved. Cousin Ronald ran in a helpless rush into the fruit machine, which he hit with a great bang, and then folded up in a heap with his eyes shut. David thought he was really hurt, until he saw Cousin Ronald open one eye to see if anyone was going to hit him again. Somebody made a playful swipe at him and he hastily shut it again. Everybody except David laughed heartily.

"Now, what did you want to ask me?" said the young man with the dragon.

David turned his red face up to him and encountered a very sympathetic smile, which soothed his shame a little. "I have to find something," he said carefully, "but I mustn't know what it is or who hid it. The three Knowing Ones said you knew where to look for it." The young man looked polite but mystified. David's heart sank. "It's important," he said. "Luke showed someone how to hide it, and he's going to have to go back to prison if I can't find it by Sunday. Are you sure you don't know about it? It belonged to the ginger-haired man – I know that because he caught Luke last Thursday and asked him about it."

"O – oh!" said the young man, and it was clear he now knew what David was talking about. "That," he said. He looked extremely unhappy. David could tell that his question had brought up a whole number of things the young man would much rather not remember. "If I'd known that was what – oh, it's not your fault, I suppose. Do you know my name?"

"No," said David.

"Then I can tell you that I took it," said the young man.

"But I don't know where it is. I gave it to – to a lady to hide."

"And where is she – this lady?" David asked.

The young man hesitated. "I'm not sure," he said sadly. "But I think if you went to Thunderly Hill you might find news of her."

"The hospital?" said Alan. "She ill then?"

"I don't think so," the young man was saying, when there was a stirring among the other young men. He turned round, and so did David, and there was Mr Wedding standing by the fruit machine, looking rather troubled. The young man with the dragon seemed unhappier than ever. "Oh, hallo, sir," he said.

"So you took it, did you?" said Mr Wedding. "I begin to understand. Why I didn't see it was you before, I can't think. Whose idea was it? Yours or hers?"

"Mine," said the young man. David knew he was lying. So did Mr Wedding.

"Hers, I see," he said. And he waited for the young man to say more.

The young man's face became even more unhappy. He looked away from Mr Wedding and stared at the painted dragon coiled round his arm. At length he said, "She came and asked me to steal it. Afterwards – when I thought everything was over."

"What? She came *here*?" Mr Wedding said sharply.

"No, no," said the young man. "I was on my way here. But she stopped me. She said it was the least I could do for her after the way I'd treated her. You see – she seemed to think it was all your fault – what had happened – and she said I owed her some revenge." He ran his finger along the coils of the dragon. "I don't see what else I could have done," he said awkwardly, "except agree. And I was about the only person who could have got it for her."

"So you were," Mr Wedding said dryly. "Why did you tell David Thunderly Hill?"

"She told me," said the young man unhappily, "that she was going back to – where I found her – afterwards. Wasn't that right?"

"Yes, you were right," said Mr Wedding. "Though you weren't supposed to know even that much." The young man looked desperately unhappy. Mr Wedding, seeing it, put his hand on his shoulder. "It's all over," he said. "Long ago." Although this did not seem to comfort the young man much, David could see Mr Wedding meant it kindly. He could see this young man meant a great deal to Mr Wedding, possibly more than all the other young men put together. And David, who up till then had not thought of himself as liking Mr Wedding particularly, wished with all his heart that he could be as valuable to him as the young man with the dragon round his arm.

Still sadly, the young man wished David luck and went back to his pintable. Mr Wedding said: "I'll meet you at Thunderly Hill, David," and left the hall.

David looked at Alan, and both of them turned rather dubiously to the collapsed heap of Cousin Ronald.

Two young men were bending over him. "What's up with this old geezer?" one of them asked David. David knew at once that he was just an ordinary young man, nothing to do with Mr Wedding or the others.

"Somebody hit him," Alan said.

"Yours, is he?" said the second young man. "Like us to help him to the First Aid post for you?"

"Could you help him across the bridge?" David said. "Our car's there."

"Wherever you like," they said obligingly, and they heaved Cousin Ronald up and marched him out of the hall. Cousin Ronald moaned and sagged. By daylight he did look battered, and the young men exclaimed over it. That made Cousin Ronald sag and moan even more. David could see that Alan knew Cousin Ronald was making the most of his hurts, and he was ashamed of him again. He had not realised that Cousin Ronald was so like Uncle Bernard.

When they came to the bridge, Cousin Ronald drew himself up with great dignity and said he could walk by himself. He added pathetically that if he took David's arm he could make it to the car. Rather grudgingly, David let him take hold of his arm and thanked the kindly young men, which Cousin Ronald had forgotten to do, and he and Alan took Cousin Ronald the rest of the way.

Astrid and Luke were at a table outside the pub, and the man with ginger hair was there too. He had his elbows on the back of Luke's chair. They were clearly enjoying themselves. Luke was finishing a vast ice-cream with chocolate sauce, which he told David later was probably his seventh, possibly his eighth. They looked up when Cousin Ronald approached between David and Alan. The ginger-haired man bit his lip in order not to laugh. Luke did laugh.

"Oh dear!" said Astrid. "What happened? Didn't they tell you where the——?"

"*Watch it!*" said both her companions.

"And you've cut your lip, David," said Astrid.

"Made you run the gauntlet, did they?" said the man with ginger hair. "Did he tell you after that?"

"Yes," said David. "Thunderly Hill. There's a lady——"

He was interrupted by a roar of delighted laughter from the ginger-haired man and Luke, and Luke cried out: "So that's it!"

"I can help you there," said the ginger-haired man.

"But David," said Luke, grinning wickedly, "you must get your cousin Ronald to hospital. He looks in a very poor way to me."

"I don't mind telling you," said Cousin Ronald, sinking dramatically into a chair, "that I've had the most awful shock. Who are these people, Astrid? We were set upon by a band of appalling roughs in an amusement arcade. Of course, I had to put myself in front of the two youngsters and take the brunt of the attack, and I got very truly mauled. But I couldn't let them beat up the boys, could I?"

Alan's mouth came open, but he was speechless. Luke's face grew redder and redder and he snorted quietly into his ice-cream. Astrid looked from Alan to David.

"Tiresome for you," she said. "Do you boys want an ice-cream?"

"So I think," said Cousin Ronald, peevish at not getting the right reaction, "that I ought to go to Thunderly Hill at once, in case I've suffered some internal injury."

"Quite right," said the ginger-haired man gravely.

"When the boys have had their ices," said Astrid. "You can wait ten minutes, can't you?"

"I doubt it," Cousin Ronald said anxiously, and Luke choked. David thumped him on the back.

Alan, with a long, wondering stare at Cousin Ronald, said he thought he would go home now.

"Not till you've had an ice-cream," said Astrid. "Something tells me you've earned it."

"What about me?" said Cousin Ronald.

"She'll buy you one too, if you ask," Luke said politely.

But Cousin Ronald insisted more and more loudly that he needed a doctor. Astrid gave Alan the money for an ice-cream and Alan left – in a mixture of embarrassment and disgust, David suspected. The ginger-haired man bought David an ice-cream, which turned out to be the best he had ever tasted, and he left also, saying he would see them at Thunderly Hill. Luke and Astrid loaded Cousin Ronald tenderly into the Mini and they set off.

As David sat beside Luke in the back seat, enjoying the ice-cream, Luke said: "This part's in my control, David. I promise I'll make it as easy for you as I can."

"Thanks," David said. "Do you think I'm going to find it in Thunderly Hill?"

"I should be very surprised if you didn't," said Luke.

"But," said David, "how shall I know that it's *it* when I see it?"

Luke thought. "If it's where I think it is," he said, "you'll know it because it's the odd thing out. Everything else will be rather different."

"That means I'm going to look it right in the face and not see it," said David. "I knew it!"

"I hope not," said Luke. "My word, I hope not! Perhaps I'd better get the owner to give you a hint of some kind."

Thunderly Hill Hospital was on the outskirts of Ashbury, built in the grounds of somewhere much older, and the old gardens were still kept up, so that they drove among flowers and lawns under a streaky blue fair-weather sky to find this mysterious lady. David asked where she was.

"Through the building," said Luke. "Let's help the poor crippled relative in first."

Cousin Ronald had acquired an artistic limp. He needed to acquire it, as Luke unkindly said, because the drive had revived him completely. Apart from a sweetly ripening black eye, he was right as rain. But he would not admit it. He had Luke and David support him on either side into a large clean hall full of unwell people waiting for doctors. There he told them irritably to leave him be. They left him sitting on a bench beside Astrid, who was evidently not enjoying herself now.

"I wish they'd hit him twice as hard!" said David.

Luke briskly led the way to a door which said *Visitors Only*. "Leave it, David," he said, pushing this door open. "If he chooses to make a fool of himself, it's nothing to do with you."

"You didn't hear the way they jeered in that hall," David retorted.

"But I can imagine," Luke said, setting out down a long corridor smelling of hospital. "They're like that. But they weren't jeering at you or Alan, were they? To hear you, you'd think you were your Cousin Ronald's Siamese twin."

David laughed, and felt a good deal less sore about it. He fell into step beside Luke. They wheeled smartly at the corner and strode down another corridor, past stacks of cylinders, trolleys, and dark brown doors labelled *E.C.G. This Way, Ear, Nose and Throat, Nightingale Ward* and so on. Half way along, David found the ginger-haired man walking beside them.

"I am going right, aren't I?" Luke asked him. "It's such a long time since I was here."

"Quite right," said the man. "You want Firestone Ward these days. And you'd better have these, in case someone asks you what you're doing."

He handed David and Luke each a round metal disc with *Firestone 7* stamped on it. David turned his over and found it said *Visitor Admit One* on the other side.

"Ah," said Luke. "Official stuff. By the way, can you give David some kind of hint or sign? He's afraid he won't recognise the thing when he sees it."

"I've been wondering," said the ginger-haired man. "I think he will, but to be on the safe side, David, if you think you've found it, look at that disc. If you have got it, you'll see the right word under the name of the ward. If there's nothing, you have to look again."

They walked on. David was expecting to see Mr Wedding too, but though they passed a number of people – one on a trolley being put into a lift marked *Operating Theatre* – none of them was Mr Wedding. And at the end of the next long corridor was a brown door marked *Firestone Ward*.

The ginger-haired man pushed it open for them. "I'll see you," he said. "Do your best for him, Luke." The door bumped shut in front of him and left David and Luke on their own.

The door led straight on to a hillside covered with pale grass. All round and very near, big purple-grey clouds came driving past and shed gusts of small icy drops on Luke and David. The grass bent and whistled in the wind, but, in spite of this it was not cold, because the hillside was on fire. David thought they were on the edge of some great forest fire. The flames were fully twenty feet high, forked, and fierce orange. They bent under the gusting wind, streaming across the sky, roaring and crackling, shedding pieces of themselves into the clouds, hissing in the rain, and leaping up more fiercely after each wet gust. At any moment it looked as if the whole hillside would be burning and David and Luke forced back through the hospital door again. The grass in front of them caught, in little running flames, and David put his hand on the door, ready to push it open again. Then came another gust of rain. The great flames leant and roared. The flames in the grass died into blue smouldering and left the grass none the worse for having been alight. The tall flames stood straight again and stayed where they were at the brow of the hill.

"Why didn't the grass catch?" David asked. "Is it too wet?"

"No," said Luke. "This fire is something of a special job. It won't move and it only consumes itself." He was looking uphill much as he had looked at the burning building, gently and fiercely, with the flames reflected in his red-brown eyes.

"Did you do it?" David asked.

Luke smiled. "Long ago. Yes. And it's going to burn to the end of time, and maybe beyond that."

David began to suspect what he might be in for. "Where do I have to go?" he asked.

"Through, I'm afraid," said Luke. "The whole lot is beyond time, you see, and I'm sure that's where it is. I can't put the flames out for you, but I can help you get through. Do you want to go now?"

"Yes," said David, knowing that the longer he stood and looked the more horrifying the flames would seem.

They climbed the hill together. The rain seemed warm and the heat from the flames reddened David's face, while Luke's became narrow, white and exultant. But it did not seem too hot to bear. Even when David was standing right beside the fire, looking into the whirling, changing heart of it, he was no more than uncomfortably hot. He looked at Luke to ask him why and saw that Luke had gone small and pale and strained.

"Not too hot are you?" said Luke.

"No," said David.

"Then go now, if you're going," said Luke. "I can't hold this heat for ever." He dropped to a crouch on the grass and David could see him shaking slightly with some huge hidden effort.

"Thanks," he said. With his arms across his head and face, rather as Alan had run the gauntlet, he plunged forward into the fire. He heard his hair frizzle. He could see smoke coming from the soles of his shoes as he trod the red-hot ground, and he smelt his clothes burning, but he still felt no more than rather too hot. There was none of the pain of burning that he had been dreading. "Perhaps I'm going to die without feeling it," he thought, and he was very grateful to Luke.

Then the flames parted ahead and he was through. Or rather, he was inside, in a hot, lurid cave surrounded by racing flames. Above, he saw a snap of stormy sky from time to time, but mostly the flames arched across and hid everything else. Dazzled by the glare and constant movement, David looked round. There seemed to be a tomb in front of him left over from a church – the tall square kind that has a statue lying on top. Otherwise, apart from a circle of grass, there was nothing else there.

"That grave, I suppose," David said to himself, and he went over to it.

It was not strictly a tomb. It was more a heap of rocks piled up to mark the top of the hill and now holding the statue. David looked down at the statue and, with a jump of horror, found it was a body. It lay on its back, as statues do on tombs, and it had been arranged so that one hand had been clasped round a queer old spear with a wide flat head which the flames made the colour of copper. The other hand was empty, but it looked as if it ought to have been holding something too. The body was wearing queer old armour, not quite like that of a knight of old, but not unlike, and the flames made that look copper too. David guessed that if whoever it was had been alive and standing up, he would have been as tall as Mr Wedding.

Then he looked on to the body's face and found it was a lady. Somehow that upset him. It was not simply that she was dead without reason and lying in the middle of timeless flames: it was that she had the most beautiful face he had ever seen. Even with her eyes shut and red in the flames she was beautiful. In a way, she reminded David a little of the lady who had driven Mr Wedding's car, except that this dead face was full of living feelings. It was a face that had no business to be dead. David gazed at it, and it dawned on him that he had never seen anyone look so sad. When the lady died, she must have been more unhappy than he had known anyone could be.

It seemed such a pity that David put out his hand and gently touched the lady's hair, which spread out in long twisted strands from her strange helmet. It might have been brown hair, but the flames made it seem coppery. As he touched it, he knew she was alive. There was a warmth about her that did not come from the fire. So he put his knuckles to her face and gave it a gentle push.

The lady did not move. Wondering why not, David looked at her chest to see if she was breathing. Because of the armour she was wearing, he was quite unable to tell. But there was a very strange object lying across her chest, now he came to look. It looked a bit like a pick-axe and seemed to be made of stone – anyway it was made of something the flames did not turn coppery. The axe-part was blunt and square at one end and curved to a rough point at the other. It had a hole in the centre of it through which the handle was slotted, and the two parts were tied together with a mass of black thongs, but, David thought, it would not have been much use as a pick because the handle was so short. There were strange writings or signs carved into both blade and handle. Everything about it suggested that it was much older than the rest of the lady's equipment.

Luke had said the thing would be the odd thing out. David said "Of course!" and was just about to snatch up the pick-axe triumphantly, when he stopped and thought. It would do no good to come away with the wrong thing. That would be all his trouble for nothing, and Luke dragged off to a worse prison than before. He took the hospital disc out of his pocket to make sure.

157

Visitor Admit One, it said. David turned it over. The number had vanished from the other side. It now read *Firestone* and, underneath, HAMMER.

David looked uncertainly at the pick-axe again. Yes, the blunt end could be a hammer – it must be a hammer – if the disc said hammer, then it was a hammer and the thing he had been looking for. But the reason for his hesitation had nothing to do with that. Of course it was a hammer, and he knew who the man was who owned it now. The trouble was, he knew who Luke was too, and he would never be able to think of Luke in the same way again.

The flames blurred a little in front of David as he reached out to pick the hammer up. Looking at the lady's unhappy face, he thought he knew a little what she felt like – just a little. But why she should lie here so sad was still a mystery to him.

The hammer was unbelievably heavy. David had to use both hands and exert all his strength to lift it. As he hauled it away across the lady's chest, he wondered why she did not move, when a great weight like that was taken off her. But she never stirred. Staggering backwards with the hammer in his arms, David thought that at least she could breathe more easily now. He meant to look if she was, but the hammer was impossible to carry as he had it, and for a while he could think of nothing but how to stop it slipping through his arms and crushing his foot. In the end, when his arms were weak and aching, he thought of hooking the curved end over one shoulder and supporting the handle in both hands. Like that he could carry it.

Then he took a last look at the sleeping lady. She had not moved. Her look of sadness had not changed, but her chest was gently rising and falling. Perhaps she was more peaceful. Full of bewildered sadness himself, David turned and trod heavily in among the flames. They whirled round him like a hot blizzard, but this time he was thinking of other things and hardly noticed them.

When he came out on the hillside, the storm had died down and there was a sunset gathering. Luke was crouching just below him looking tired to death, ten times more tired than he had looked after Mr Wedding caught him. And as soon as he set eyes on him, David discovered that knowing all about someone need not change your feelings at all. Luke might be lord of fire and master of mischief. He might have done a number of appalling things and be going to do more before he was through. But David was simply very glad to see him again, and extremely sorry that he had been so slow fetching the hammer that he had tired Luke out.

"I've got it," he called out.

Luke's red head jerked up and he gave David a big tired smile. "Thank goodness!" he said. "Get down the hill a bit and then I can let it go."

David slithered under the weight of the hammer ten yards or so down the slope. Then he felt a sudden blare of heat on his back and turned to see Luke getting up slowly and stretching as if he were stiff.

"I was afraid you'd been burnt," Luke called across the roaring of the flames. He came slithering stiffly downhill, and there was no doubt he was quite as glad to see David as David was to see him. "I kept remembering you were only human," he said, "and I was scared stiff you'd had it. I kept telling myself that once anyone leaves time there's no telling how long they'll be, but I'd stopped believing it by this time."

"How long was I?" asked David.

"Well," Luke said, rather apologetically, "it's Sunday evening now."

"Sunday!" David exclaimed, and could think of

nothing but Luke crouching and quelling the heat of the fire for nearly two days and a night.

"I know," said Luke. "What will Aunt Dot say?"

"Idiot! I wasn't—" David began, but he was distracted by the sight of black pinions spread like fingers against the flames.

"Can I tell him you've got it?" called the raven, wheeling above Luke's head.

"Yes," said David.

The bird swooped up and away. It must have been going to Mr Wedding, because there was a shout from downhill just then and David saw the owner of the hammer running delightedly up the slope towards him. David was very glad to see him. His shoulder was aching badly from the weight of the thing by this time. He slithered down to meet the ginger-haired man.

"Here you are," he said. "Your name's Thor, isn't it?"

"That's right," the man said, smiling. "Thank you." He took the hammer off David's shoulder with no trouble at all and hooked it on to his own shoulder in just the same way. He looked familiar and comfortable doing it. "That feels better," said Thor. "I've missed the feel."

Then the tall people began to come up the hill and congratulate David. The Frys came, large and laughing, and Mr Chew, who wrung his hand painfully and said: "Well, I didn't think you'd do it." Numbers of others came too and they all said something to David, though not all of them said anything to Luke. Thor did, and the red-headed girl, who could hardly wait to thank David before she threw her arms round Luke. Then Mr Wedding came up the hill with the raven on his shoulder. He smiled at Luke over the girl's head and then at David.

"Thank you, David," he said. "It's always a better bargain when we're on the same side."

For a moment, David had the idea Mr Wedding might be looking at him in something the same way that he had looked at the young man with the dragon, but before he could be sure, Astrid came rushing up, stumbling in very silly shoes, shoved Mr Wedding aside and flung both arms round David. Not being used to it, David felt very shy.

"Oh, I'm so glad!" said Astrid. "I was afraid you'd gone for good. You smell like burnt toast, did you know?"

"I can't help that," said David. Mr Wedding laughed.

Thor rescued David by bending down and saying: "Would you like to see what this hammer can do?"

"Yes, please," said David.

"Stand back then," said Thor.

While they retreated down the hillside, Thor was looking for a suitable spot on the ground. When he had found it, he stood back, gigantic and dark against the flames, and taking the hammer off his shoulder he swung it over his head and down on to the hillside. The shock shook the hill like an exploding shell. Blue lightning struck down in the place the hammer hit, with a vicious sizzle, whitening Thor and making the flames look pale. The most tremendous peal of thunder followed, clap after shrill clap, each with its following train of crashes. Then the rain came down, drenchingly, and even the immortal flames bent under it.

David was dazzled and deafened and let Astrid and Luke pull him downhill without a word. "You'll catch your deaths," said Astrid. Her Mini was parked at the bottom of the hill and Astrid tore open the door and bundled them both in. They watched the rest of the storm from behind the windscreen wipers, and Mr Wedding watched it too from the front passenger seat, with the raven making contented nibbling noises from his shoulder.

When the thunder had abated a little, Astrid said:

"You'll never guess what's happened, David. Dot and Bernard and Ronald have run for it."

"Run for what?" said David.

"Run away, silly," said Astrid. "The police think they're out of the country by now. That's how much they were worried about you being missing. Or me either, for that matter."

"But why?" said David. Of all the unlikely things he could think of it was Cousin Ronald going abroad with a black eye or Uncle Bernard going at all.

Astrid explained, with some help from Mr Wedding. It seemed that for some years, though neither Astrid nor David had known, David's three relations had been living very comfortably by spending money that was really David's. "Funny to think this Mini belongs to you," Astrid said. There had been much gossip about it in the neighbourhood, but no one had liked to do anything about it until Mr Fry – the real old Mr Fry – came to live at the end of the road. Mr Fry had been a solicitor. Even before he met David, he felt something should be done and, once he had met David, he began to investigate very vigorously indeed.

"He said he took you up as a hobby," said Astrid. "That's the way he talks. But don't ask me to explain too much because he'd talk the hind leg off a mule and then tie it in knots. All I know is that Mr Wedding gave Mr Fry a few hints and it turned out that Ronald and Bernard have been up to no end of swindles with this money of yours and broke the law in twenty different pieces."

Thanks to Mr Wedding, Mr Fry had enough proof by Saturday to go to the police. But again, perhaps thanks to Mr Wedding, though Mr Wedding was evasive about this, Cousin Ronald had got wind of it.

"So they took off last night in a taxi," said Astrid, "leaving you missing and me to fend for myself. And that was a weight off my mind, David, because it had been bothering me that you weren't related to me, so I couldn't legally march off with you. But I don't think any one could blame us now. Roll on Alan's Mum, eh?"

"Brilliant!" said David. He could think of no other word for it.

Then he found he was aching to ask a hundred questions – not about Cousin Ronald, Uncle Bernard and Aunt Dot, but about all the other things. He was a little shy of asking, however, now he knew that Mr Wedding, sitting beside Astrid in the Mini, must be none other than Woden, All Father and Hidden One, and might not choose to answer questions. David managed to stop himself asking about Luke. He remembered now that Luke had been put in prison for killing someone called Baldur. And he thought he knew about Thor, and the Frys, and Mr Chew, who had given his name to Tuesday. But there was one thing he just had to ask.

"Er – Mr Wedding, who was the young man with the dragon?"

Mr Wedding turned his head and seemed surprised. "Don't you know him? They called him Siegfried, or Sigurd in the North – a dragon-killer and a distant relative of mine. He was very famous in his day."

"Oh," said David. "Then the lady in there—?" He looked up the hill, through the streaming window of the car. The everlasting flames were bitten into ragged shapes by the rain.

"Brunhilda," said Luke. "You must have heard of her."

"She's also related to me," said Mr Wedding.

"Yes, but—" said David, and hardly knew which question to ask first.

"The story," said Mr Wedding, "is told in various ways. But the main part is always the same: Siegfried went through those flames and won Brunhilda, and then pretended that it was another man who did it. Brunhilda married this other man, and Siegfried married the man's sister. Then Brunhilda found the truth. She had Siegfried killed and left the world herself. She was not really mortal, you see."

David was still puzzled. "Did he – Sigurd – like the other lady more, then? He didn't seem to – just now, at Wallsey, I mean."

"No. He was mistaken," said Mr Wedding.

"Was that mistake your doing, by any chance?" Luke asked shrewdly. "Brunhilda seemed to think it was when she came to see me in prison." Mr Wedding thoughtfully stroked the raven and said nothing. "I thought as much," said Luke. "Their children might have threatened your power, eh? But she found another way of cutting your powers down when she took the hammer into those flames with her. Am I right?"

Mr Wedding sighed. "More or less. These things have to be, Luke. We've been in a poor way, these last thousand years, without the hammer. Other beliefs have conquered us very easily. But now, thanks to David, we'll have our full strength for the final battle." He turned and looked at Luke, smiling slightly. Luke looked back and did not smile at all.

It came home to David that Luke and Mr Wedding were going to be on opposite sides, when that final battle came. He was still trying to get used to this idea when the storm died away. The rain cleared, leaving a yellow evening sky with a rainbow mistily against it. Thor came down the hill, soaking wet and laughing, with the hammer hooked on his shoulder again.

"This is where we say good-bye," said Mr Wedding. "I shall see you again, though." He opened the car door and got out. "Coming, Luke?"

"I'll stay for the moment," Luke said, nestling comfortably in the corner of the back seat. Mr Wedding laughed and shut the door.

David climbed over to the front seat while Astrid started the engine. "Well, David," she said. "That's that."

David looked at her to remind her that Luke was still there. There was the same expression on Astrid's face that he had seen on the lady's in the flames. David was rather surprised that he should be sad. Getting rid of Cousin Ronald seemed to him a thing to rejoice at. He looked away at first, because he thought that kind of sadness must be private. Then he thought of that other lady. He had wanted to do something for her because she was sad, and he knew he never would be able to. But he might manage to comfort Astrid.

"What's the matter?" he said.

"Oh, what a comfort you're here again," she said. "Nothing you can help about, David. Wouldn't you say it was worth it, to be really happy for a while, even if you knew you were going to end up sad ever after?"

David thought of the lady in the flames, asleep and sad for ever, and did not know. "What do you think?" he asked Luke.

"Tell you on Monday," said Luke. "I have to go to sleep now. It's urgent."

Also by Diana Wynne Jones

FIRE AND HEMLOCK

Suddenly Polly begins to remember . . .

Halloween, nine years ago. She gatecrashed a funeral party at the big house. She met Tom Lynn for the first time. And he gave her the strange photograph of the hemlock flowers and the fire.

But what has happened in the years between? Why has Polly erased Tom from her own mind and the rest of the world as well? How could she have forgotten him when he had meant so much to her? And how can she unlock her memory, before her quest becomes a matter of life or death . . .

A fascinating story of intrigue and sorcery.

Diana Wynne Jones

A TALE OF TIME CITY

Vivian has been kidnapped! She's sure that Jonathan and Sam have whisked her away to a city of the future. But Time City exists outside time and space – though its inhabitants, as Vivian discovers, couldn't be more human.

Trying to get back home, Vivian becomes entangled in the plight of the crumbling Time City. A desperate hunt begins through time to find its builder, the legendary Faber John, and his four precious caskets. But someone else is determined to find him first – someone who is spreading chaos throughout history in an attempt to destroy the city. Is it the dreaded Time Lady? Or an unknown adversary?

A Selected List of Fiction from Mammoth

While every effort is made to keep prices low, it is sometimes necessary to increase prices at short notice. Mandarin Paperbacks reserves the right to show new retail prices on covers which may differ from those previously advertised in the text or elsewhere.

The prices shown below were correct at the time of going to press.

☐	7497 0978 2	**Trial of Anna Cotman**	Vivien Alcock £2.50
☐	7497 0712 7	**Under the Enchanter**	Nina Beachcroft £2.50
☐	7497 0106 4	**Rescuing Gloria**	Gillian Cross £2.50
☐	7497 0035 1	**The Animals of Farthing Wood**	Colin Dann £3.50
☐	7497 0613 9	**The Cuckoo Plant**	Adam Ford £3.50
☐	7497 0443 8	**Fast From the Gate**	Michael Hardcastle £1.99
☐	7497 0136 6	**I Am David**	Anne Holm £2.99
☐	7497 0295 8	**First Term**	Mary Hooper £2.99
☐	7497 0033 5	**Lives of Christopher Chant**	Diana Wynne Jones £2.99
☐	7497 0601 5	**The Revenge of Samuel Stokes**	Penelope Lively £2.99
☐	7497 0344 X	**The Haunting**	Margaret Mahy £2.99
☐	7497 0537 X	**Why The Whales Came**	Michael Morpurgo £2.99
☐	7497 0831 X	**The Snow Spider**	Jenny Nimmo £2.99
☐	7497 0992 8	**My Friend Flicka**	Mary O'Hara £2.99
☐	7497 0525 6	**The Message**	Judith O'Neill £2.99
☐	7497 0410 1	**Space Demons**	Gillian Rubinstein £2.50
☐	7497 0151 X	**The Flawed Glass**	Ian Strachan £2.99

All these books are available at your bookshop or newsagent, or can be ordered direct from the publisher. Just tick the titles you want and fill in the form below.

Mandarin Paperbacks, Cash Sales Department, PO Box 11, Falmouth, Cornwall TR10 9EN.

Please send cheque or postal order, no currency, for purchase price quoted and allow the following for postage and packing:

UK including BFPO   £1.00 for the first book, 50p for the second and 30p for each additional book ordered to a maximum charge of £3.00.

Overseas including Eire   £2 for the first book, £1.00 for the second and 50p for each additional book thereafter.

NAME (Block letters) ....

ADDRESS ....

....

☐ I enclose my remittance for ....

☐ I wish to pay by Access/Visa Card Number

Expiry Date